FIREWYRM

Worldship Files – \

By Erik Schubach

For Nikki, you will be missed.

CHAPTER 1
We Didn't Start The Fire

One of the drawbacks of being an officer of the Enforcer's Brigade on the Worldship Leviathan is that it seems you are always on call. You patrol the quad of your home ring and police the citizens who run afoul of the law and investigate any cases in your area.

On the positive side, you have full autonomy, and though most enforcers work with partners, other enforcers aren't brought in on your cases unless you called them in for backup. You handle all aspects of your cases up until your suspects go before a judge. Once you made that hand-off, you are free to go back to your normal duties.

But there are a handful of times where, no matter what you were doing, whether you were in the middle of an investigation or just trying to enjoy your off-hours, that you dropped everything to run to the aid of the citizens of the Leviathan.

Two scenarios come quickly to mind. First was a hull breach in the Worldship, whether in one of the habitation rings, the trunk, or the Heart of the multigenerational vessel we call our world. The other was, in my opinion, even more terrifying. Fire.

In a hull breach, the danger of being sucked out into hard vacuum was frightening, but the series of blast doors in every section of the ship limited that possibility by sealing off any sections that were exposed to vacuum. And in the case of complete power failure in those sections, the blast doors failed closed, which means if power was cut, the artificial gravity, created by the centrifugal force of the spinning rings, pulled the doors down to seal.

Infinitely worse was a fire in the enclosed environment of a ship in space. It could spread out of control, consuming vital oxygen that is needed to keep us all alive. And if the fire spread from the skin and bulkhead corridors and out into the open spaces in a ring, consuming green spaces that helped to generate oxygen to replace what is lost is such a catastrophe, thousands of lives could be at risk.

The last time this occurred was in the C-Ring of Delta-Stack three hundred years ago, when the parkland area called The Strip had caught fire, burning all two hundred square acres before emergency containment crews got it under control. The entire ring needed emergency evac and three dozen souls were lost. It took three months for the air scrubbers to make the atmosphere breathable again, and almost three decades to repair all of the structural damage.

I swear that C-Ring Delta still smells of hints of smoke whenever I have to visit it. The entire Delta-Stack was reduced to eighty-five percent of normal atmospheric oxygen saturation for nine months before the organics generated enough oxygen to replace what was lost and replenish their reserves.

I shuddered at the thought as I put my cards on the table and stood, looking around at the others as the alarm klaxons sounded.

Mac's lips were a tight line on his face, worry in his eyes. He was the supposedly human captain of the Remnant vessel Underhill, and I suspected he was a whole lot more as well. Mir, the human woman who went full cyber with total body replacement with her mirrored skin, stood with Jane, the cute Faun madame of the Underhill's brothel.

The last occupant of the captain's cabin where we were having our weekly game of Quads down-ring on the Underhill, where it and the other Remnant ships docked to her where she occupied one of the airlock docking ports on the skin of the Beta-Stack's D-Ring, was Ben. Another human Enforcer like me. He moonlighted at the brothel here to supplement the meager income we made as Enforcers.

I snapped up my goggles from the side table as Jane and Mir left swiftly to see to the people in the brothel. The corridor outside the cabin looked to be chaos with people running and yelling as they either ran back to the world through the airlock or to their quarters here on the ancient construction and engineering vessel which had helped to build the Leviathan over five thousand years ago. That the Underhill or any other Remnants were still space worthy was a miracle in itself.

My goggles, well they technically belonged to my ex, Myra, had a full tech pack like my armor which I was sorely missing just then. Myra flew with the Ready Squadron, the ace fliers who were always on point, flying in front of the Leviathan, and clearing a path through any asteroid, meteor or comet debris which crossed our path. Blowing anything larger than a Hel Ball into smaller pieces that couldn't penetrate the armor of the Skin. So the goggles, even though they were twenty-six years old, almost matched the tech of my new experimental armor.

With a thought, the virtual screens bloomed in my vision as I asked quickly, "Mother?"

The AI of the Leviathan answered me in the stilted, mechanical tone she used when people other than me could hear her. "Fire in Alpha-Stack B-Ring, Priority Orange. All emergency crews from all stacks ordered to respond."

Priority Orange? I felt the blood drain from my face. By the gods...

The A and B rings of each stack held vast forests like were rumored to have existed on the Ground, under Open Air, where machines and the ship's oxygen processing systems were not needed to keep us breathing, to keep us alive. But I have questioned if they were simply rumors after speaking to a couple of the Old Earth Fae who say they were there on the day five thousand years ago when the Leviathan left the orbit of that dying planet.

And Fae... well everyone knows that the Greater Fae cannot lie. Which makes them the best deceivers of all the races, they can spin the truth to make you believe anything they wish and not tell a single lie while doing it. And being in the Brigade, I've seen the outer rings, the lush forests and villages, and rivers that they modeled after Earth. I can almost imagine what it would be like if those forests went on forever instead of being constrained to just a mile wide strip in the fifty-mile diameter torus of the A-Rings. And B-Rings, while still mind-boggling huge, weren't quite as heavily forested, but they were still over two-thirds covered in green spaces and crops.

Code-Orange was just about the worst-case scenario, it meant that, like the incident in the Delta-Stack's C-Ring, the fire had breached the bulkhead and was threatening the green spaces. If the forests caught... well, this could kill the entire Alpha-Stack.

I started toward the door. "Emergency travel time?" I already knew, and it made me feel useless. I'd have to travel to a spoke, then down to the trunk and over to the Alpha-Stack and then up-ring to B.

"Using emergency transit lanes, forty-one minutes, fifteen seconds," Mother replied

I reached the door and paused and asked, "Jump Pods?" In a fire, forty-one minutes was forty lifetimes.

The tin voice responded, "Including transit time to the nearest Jump Terminal, and four jumps. Twenty-seven minutes, two seconds."

"Fuck."

Mac cleared his throat behind me and I looked back, and the man tapped the air in front of his eyes. I reached up absently to touch the goggles I wore and got his meaning. Again, my blood ran cold but just nodded thanks to him.

He followed on my heels as I dashed out into the corridor. "Aft docking port is two levels down."

We pushed through the diminishing foot traffic toward the lift bank and ladders down instead of turning toward the airlock to the world. We had to move aside as a centaur trotted past in a panic. Mac shared as we slid down the first ladder, "I'd fly you there myself, but the other remnants who are docked with me would have to detach and move to a safe distance, you don't have that kind of time.

I had no doubt that he would. I started to ask Mother as I cringed, "Connect me with..." She was, as always, two steps ahead of me. To someone else, it would likely be unnerving if Mother anticipated their needs before you even voiced them, but she has always had my back.

A familiar voice from my past, frosty and devoid of emotion, spoke before I finished my request, "Knith? Knith Shade? I'm a little busy right now, lady. Most of the Ready Fleet is being recalled for an emergency in..."

I cut her off. "Fire in Alpha-B. Need transport from the Underhill on the Skin of Beta-D."

She lost the cold in her tone and was serious as a heart attack at the mention of the fire. "Underhill? Mother, coord... ah, thank you. That old Remnant wreck? What are you... never mind, ETA two minutes."

Mac pointed to the end of a corridor with a metal grid floor, seeing the wide red and white warning stripes around the airlock door, and the blue light indicating hard vacuum on the other side of the double set of doors.

I nodded my thanks, and he handed me my bombardier jacket which, technically was Myra's too. Wait a minute, Mir had just been wearing this so we didn't see her cards reflected on her chest when she left the card game to go to the brothel.

So how did he... magic?

He didn't even have the common decency to wait for me to accuse him of being King Oberon before he spun on his heel and headed back down the corridor. "Godspeed, Knith, things are about to get... interesting. Where there's flame, there isn't necessarily fire."

Ok, why did that just scare me as much as the alarm klaxons? Did I want things to get interesting? Mother, back to her normal chirpy and emotive state said to me, "Why does that man give me the chills?"

"Can an AI get chills?"

"Focus, Knith."

"Right. Ok, ETA?"

"Fifteen seconds."

I nodded. "Great, and I'll need my..."

She sighed at me and said in a patient tone, "I've already had your armor sent in the tubes. It'll be there when you are."

I loved how she anticipated my needs.

The transit tubes were a high-speed delivery system that could get packages delivered even from the greatest distance, Alpha-Stack A-Ring to Delta-Stack A-Ring in just a couple of minutes. And emergency services had their own set of tubes that paralleled the system.

I saw something swoop down through the windows of the airlock and smoothly contact the docking port with barely a sound translating through the ship's hull. I smiled weakly to myself. Myra was one of the best pilots in Ready Squadron, an amazing feat as she, like me, was only human. Most of the other preternatural species that inhabited the Worldship had better reflexes and situational awareness than us.

The lights cycled on the controls until they showed three greens of a hard seal and pressurization. I cycled the inner doors and stepped inside, and once the doors cycled shut, the outer airlock doors cycled and a familiar figure stood in the opening, her tail twitched with annoyance.

I felt almost embarrassed, not knowing what to say to her as her slitted feline eyes blinked. "Umm... hi Myra. Thank you for coming and..."

She actually hissed at me. She had always had a cyber cat fetish and was heavily modded. The only human I knew personally who had gone farther with mods than Myra was Mir. "Just get your ass into my ship and strap in. The reports on the waves sound bad."

I nodded and hustled after her into the small, sleek, two-seat

Sentinel, and strapped into the co-pilot station. She slid into the pilot's seat with the liquid grace that had attracted me to her in the first place and took her in as she disengaged the docking clamps and prepped for flight like she had done it a million times.

The soft downy fur of her feline face begged to be touched, with its calico markings. I could see where time had matured her from the young and foolish twenty-one-year-olds we had been, to a young adult of forty-six. The maturity looked good on her.

She glanced at me and did a double-take, seeing me looking her over. She slid her flight goggles on as she prompted, "Is that my old gear?"

Oh, mother fairy humper... this was embarrassing. When I was off duty and heading down-ring to the Underhill, I wore her stuff for an Irontown Grunge look so I fit in on the Remnants, since I didn't own very many civilian clothes. Until recently, the Brigade has sort of been my entire life.

I sputtered, "I, umm..."

"Don't sweat it, it looks good on you." Then she squinted at me as the ship arced smoothly away from the Underhill, leaving my stomach behind. "You look exactly the same, not a day older."

I shrugged. I had always looked young for my age, which I have always seen as a curse, as it makes it difficult to get the respect of the other Enforcers in the Brigade, add to that that I'm human, and I usually get the shit postings.

It wasn't until recently that I learned that it wasn't by accident. I was a failed experiment by the Fae, to create a Changeling, a bridge between humans and Greater Fae so that they could bring their population back up to the numbers they had after Exodus from the dying Earth. Without that bond to the magic of Old Earth, the Fae discovered they couldn't reproduce. They hope that when we arrive at our new home on Eridani Prime at the end of the Leviathan's ten thousand year journey, that the native nature magic of that planet will be enough to give them the ability again.

The Fae Princess of the Unseelie Winter Court, Aurora Ashryver, who I might possibly be in some sort of relationship with... it's still a little vague to me, had attempted to create a bridge, so that their people could reproduce by making beings that were half-human, and half-Fae, and their offspring would be fully Fae. The experiment failed. The only embryo that survived at the Beta-Stack Reproduction Clinic was, well... me.

Where she had failed to create a Changeling, she did succeed in making me sort of, more human? I was what she excitedly calls the next evolution of man. My genes are all tailored to be the best and improved versions of human, and all the shortcomings we humans have as the lesser race on the world were edited out of me. Including apparently, my lifespan.

When cells divide, the telomeres in the chromosomes shorten. This is the aging process. And when those telomeres are too short to divide, then the organism... Humans, in this case, die. Like a kill switch in computer code, Humans are programmed to die after only a hundred and fifty to two hundred years. My chromosomes have no degradation of telomeres by design.

For all intents and purposes, as long as I don't die, I had a sort of limited immortality. I healed faster than an average human, but I could still die from wounds just like any other human. It had the unfortunate side effect of leaving me looking around nineteen or twenty for the rest of my life, like the Fae. Even the oldest and most powerful of the Fae looked to be young adults unless they used a glamour spell to appear older, and they were all unnaturally attractive.

There were some perks to being a failed lab rat which almost made up for the fact that I felt just that, some lab experiment that didn't go well so I was just thrown out to fend for myself.

Being a Clinic Child, or CC, I had no family and was raised by the Reproduction Clinic. I was grown in an artificial womb with the other embryos to keep static Equilibrium of the human population.

Whenever any race's birth rates were down, the clinics... well, the clinics grew more to keep the world's population at twelve million. So I was born forty-six years ago in the clinic, and the lesser Fae nurses were responsible for giving us 'designations', our names. They were obviously bored or were of the same opinion that we nulls aren't worth their time as they gave me the Shade surname... meaning 'nobody'... since that was what we Clinic Children were, especially us Humans, nobodies. No family, no home, nothing.

Throughout my entire childhood, I grew up with that knowledge and was told how I only existed to keep a population quota and nothing I did would ever amount to anything. I pushed back and excelled in school, then the university, and then I joined the Brigade to protect people and make a difference, thumbing my nose at those who thought I was just shade.

Myra pointed at her lips, a smirk on her face. "What are those? You swore to me that you'd never get mods."

I absently reached up to touch my lips, feeling the slick and smooth translucent blue ice. "They're not a mod. I'm still one hundred percent pure human. This is Queen Mab's mark, she's apparently punishing me for some imagined insult."

Her eyes widened. "I heard about you consorting with the Greater Fae. Accusing them of murder? Only you could get away with insulting the Winter Queen."

"Hey, I just said it was an imagined slight."

"I can't see you not upsetting her in some way, Knith, it's who you are. You don't have a discretion filter installed between your brain and your mouth."

Fair point, but still. Hey.

"Hang on, hitting thrusters," Myra said.

I was pressed back in my seat under the extreme G forces of our acceleration as she flew a clean arc on a parabolic course over the Beta Stack and down toward the Alpha-Stack, without instruments. She still had the touch. She'd have us docking in less than three minutes.

I couldn't help shouting out "Yeehaaaaaw!" in my adrenaline rush. Then I asked, "Mother, some appropriate music?"

In the earpieces of the goggles, a song called We Didn't Start the Fire, by a musician named Billy Joel started blasting. Myra's cat ears twitched, then she made a motion in the air and the music blasted in the cabin. After a few bars, she asked, "What is this?"

I supplied, "I was recently introduced to the anthropological music archives, late twentieth century..."

She nodded, and bobbed to the beat, then pointed up as she rotated us on the Y-axis and I gasped at the breathtaking sight before me. I mean, I knew what the Leviathan looked like, I've seen thousands of pictures, models, holographs and the like, and could see parts of her in the roof of the world, but actually seeing her from space...

Mother, anticipating me, lowered the volume so I could appreciate the sight. Stretching off into the distance, I could see the counter-rotating stacks of the habitat rings, almost incomprehensible in scope, as light from the nebula we were flying past danced along the hull of the Leviathan like diamonds glittering in pools along her hull. The stacks were spaced evenly along the trunk of the ship, with a bulging sphere in the middle, the core or heart of the Worldship that held a seven-mile diameter asteroid inside of it which we mined for resources.

Myra reached over and gently closed my mouth which had been

hanging open. I whispered in awe, "She's beautiful."

Mother chirped out, sounding almost bashful, "Thank you, Knith."

Catching the ship AI's slip up, emoting around someone other than me and Graz, my ex looked at me then the console, brows pinched as she asked, "Mother?"

Mother responded, sounding tinny and mechanical again, "Yes Commander Udriel? Awaiting input."

Myra narrowed her eyes in a very catlike manner then sighed and addressed me, "I live for this sight. It reminds me every time I see it, just how small we are in the grand scheme of the world. It tells me there have to be gods in the heavens to have created the Leviathan."

I nodded, unable to tear my eyes from the sight, "I've never seen her like this..." This was our world, taking in the sheer scope of her made me realize the impossible undertaking our ancestors had embarked upon to save all the races of the old world, solid ground, open air, sky. Myra was right, we were all small in comparison to what was achieved to save twelve million souls from a world that was slowly being swallowed by an expanding sun.

It didn't matter who we were, Fae, shifters, Elves, Minotaurs, Vampires, and even my non-magical race, or nulls... Humans. The Leviathan was the monument to the world we left behind and served as the only world many of us short-lived species have ever known. And her beauty was beyond compare.

Then Myra was firing thrusters again sending us hurtling down toward the Alpha-Stack. The song was finishing just as we were docking at an airlock near the emergency. I noted a blemish on the hull a few dozen yards away, like the rippling diamond Skin had been charred. I assumed it was a micro-meteorite strike, nothing the Leviathan couldn't take.

Once the outer airlock doors cycled, Myra stayed behind, saying, "I've got to get back in front of the world, there's a hole in coverage since I peeled out to ferry your ass here." Then she added, "Be safe... a fire isn't anything to take chances with, Knith."

Then she added before I could thank her, "Surprisingly, it wasn't unpleasant... seeing you again."

I sighed. It was my fault we broke up. She had already got her commission as a pilot in Ready Fleet when we were finishing college. She wanted me to follow her, but I always thought the Brigade was my calling. Since the two services are always butting heads, she didn't think it would work between us if I joined the Enforcers.

As much as I thought I loved her, I knew I had to follow my heart as well, or I wouldn't be happy and that would poison our relationship. She gave me an ultimatum, her or the Brigade... I chose, she left.

Nodding, my eyes widened. "Oh, here, these are yours." I started to take off the goggles and flight jacket and she looped my hands with her tail.

She shrugged. "No, that's alright, they always looked better on you." Then she turned away and hit the door controls as she said, "Godspeed."

I turned back and gave her a sad smile through the window, placing a hand on it and mouthed, "Godspeed," to her back as she headed back to the cockpit.

Turning back to the inner doors and cycling them, I walked into chaos and smoke. Even all the way back here in Bulkhead J? I yelled above the klaxons. "Mother?"

"The closest I could route your gear is a tube port fifty yards counter-rotation," she said.

I nodded and called out as I ran that way, "Thanks." Then shouted at the panicking citizens as I ran past, "Get to safety, go down-ring to C, and emergency personnel will take care of you."

This isn't the first time I've witnessed this, there have been emergencies before, nothing as severe as fire, but some people, when they panic, they run deep into the bulkheads, toward the Skin instead of the safety of the open rings, or heading to a safe ring until the emergency is resolved.

They taught us about this in the academy, it is the fight or flight instinct that is deeply ingrained into some species. Long ago, before mankind rose to power on Earth, some races would go to ground, some literally, burrowing tunnels to get away from predators. The problem here is that that instinct could get them killed in instances like this.

I looked over to a Faun who was huddling against the bulkhead with a family of Satyrs. I needed to get to their rational minds. I crouched at the group and took the Faun's soft furred hand and placed another hand on the male Satyr's shoulder. "I need you to head counter-rotation to the next cross corridor and head out to the... hey... look at me!"

Their eyes snapped up at the forceful command, I made sure I had their attention as I said, "I need you to be brave for me, ok? I need you to get out to the open Ring, get to a spoke and head down-ring. I need you to be brave for the other Fauns and Satyrs out there who are afraid and confused. You need to bring them with you... it will be safe down in the C-Ring until we can get this fire contained."

I looked at them hopefully. "Can you do that for me? Help me get the others to safety?"

They looked apprehensive as they slowly stood, first the Faun then the Satyr nodded, letting their brains override their instinct. Then they huddled together and loped off toward the next cross corridor. Good.

We reached the tube station and I gave my voice authorization to open and just as I opened the pill-shaped capsule to retrieve my armor and weapons, a streak of light burst out of it, leaving a sparkling trail of dust.

The Sprite who was my unwanted roommate, along with her, or his family, buzzed around until it landed on my shoulder. Pronouns were always hard for me with tri-sex species like Sprites. We agreed since she had no preference, to use female pronouns since she had cute femininity to her androgyny.

She blurted, "Wooo! Now that was a rush! I gotta do that again. Have you ever ridden in one of those things? They're insanely fast! Well, of course, you haven't, you bigs can't fit. Too bad..."

I put a finger over her face, then once she stopped, and buzzed her wings in agitation, I asked, "Graz, what are you doing here? There's a fire. It's dangerous."

She crossed her arms. "What? And it's fine that you go rushing into it? Come on, we're partners. Someone's gotta watch your back or my family loses its posh quarters."

Rolling my eyes I said over the klaxons that I was getting so used to I could barely hear them now, "Heaven forbid you lose my quarters where you're crashing. At least we know you have your priorities straight."

"Well, I do sort of worry about you too, Shade. You're ok, you know, for a big null and all. Someone has to have your back."

I offered, "Mother has my back."

"Yes, I do."

"Hey, you big tin can, shush, we're talkin' here."

"Knith, if you place her back in the tube, I can route her out to hard vacuum."

Graz flipped off the nearest observation camera and I held up my hands. "Ladies! Please, there's a fire. You can squabble later."

I looked around and sighed, watching people dashing around in the smoke-filled corridor and I stripped then donned my armor and helmet, feeling much better with the reassuring weight of it and the weapons at my side. I quickly stuffed my other stuff back in the transport container and Mother sent it zipping back off to my quarters.

I said to Graz as she tucked herself into my hair at my cheek, "Seriously, why are you here? You could get hurt."

She shrugged and said, "Mother told me about the fire and how you were just running straight to it." She shrugged again and I sighed.

"Well, hang on then, no doubt things are going to get rough. First responders haven't even reached bulkhead J, so we're early to the party."

Then I was running as fast as I could toward the hotspot on the map being projected in my peripheral by the suit's heads up display. Calling out with the suit's amplifier, "Make a hole, Brigade!" Blue and amber lights of Enforcer pursuit flashed on my shoulders.

CHAPTER 2
Bad Reputation

I burst out into the open ring, first responders were arriving from all directions as the Leviathan's automated fire suppression systems were valiantly holding back a raging inferno from the edges of the forest.

"Report," I asked Mother.

She said, a touch of confusion in her tone, "Something seems to be feeding the flames, self oxygenating, and I can barely keep them from spreading farther. There's a lot of structural damage inside the bulkheads... wait... it seems to be moving like it is alive. It's about to burst out of Bulkhead A."

I looked around and saw the re-breathers being unloaded from a fire suppression team that was arriving. Mother sighed. "You still haven't reviewed the specs on your new armor, have you Knith?"

"Umm... maybe."

"Here, allow me."

My visor shot up and I held my arm up when I felt the nano-panels of the armor reconfiguring It became beefier with what looked like rough, black refractory coating on it. I heard the air inside the helmet being evacuated, but before I could panic, I could breathe again... smoke-free air and Mother was in my head saying, "This is thermal ablative mode, it can withstand up to twelve hundred degrees and will give you thirty minutes of breathable air in fire or toxic environments. You really should look over the specifications to..."

I muttered, "I know, I know. Can you save the lecture until later... mom? Get me to the fire marshal then we have to get to whatever is moving around before it breaches the bulkhead."

A light pinged on the map. Great, I had offended her, now she wasn't talking to me. I almost jumped when Graz asked from right beside my ear, "Who you talkin' to, Knith? You know one of the first signs of insanity is speaking to yourself."

I exhaled. I had already forgotten she was there, now she was sealed inside my helmet. "Just zip it Graz." Then I added, "And Mother when you decide you're talking to me again, pipe it through the internal speakers so the bug doesn't think I'm crazy."

"The bug?!"

I slapped my helmet. "Zip it!" She made a zipping motion over her lips in my peripheral vision.

Then she unzipped them to say, "You don't gotta be so..." She quickly zipped her lips again when I threatened to slap the helmet again.

The whole time this was going on, my eyes were on the ship's schematics that Mother was feeding me. She was highlighting the damaged areas, and it was frightening, whatever kind of fire this was, was burning hot enough to melt through multiple bulkheads that were thick enough to take a moderate meteorite strike.

I reached the fire marshal, who was shouting out orders. I called out, "Knith Shade, Enforcer. What can I do?"

The Minotaur woman looked me up and down and pointed back. "Crowd control! Other Enforcers are arriving now. Get those lookie-loos down-ring. Damn vacuum sucking idiots." She growled as she was looking at the readouts on a pad in front of her, "Oh space me now." Then she was yelling, "Containment, get the gods be damned magi-tech Pyre-Suits sent up here now. This monster of a fire will melt our normal MTFS gear. Get suppression teams on the perimeter and in the bulkheads to contain this beast until we can detonate a cryo-core in the heart of it."

At a thought, Mother was providing me with the specs on the MTFS gear. Their suits could only protect them up to eight hundred degrees. The Pyre-Suits could handle almost eighteen hundred. And the fire's core was burning around eleven hundred.

I placed a hand on the fire marshal's flank and she turned back toward me, her hooves clopping and tail swishing in agitation as she hissed out, "I don't have time for this, the bulkhead is on the verge of collapse, you stupid null! Every second counts."

Ignoring the insult I told her, "I can get a cryo-core in there for you. My suit can handle the heat, twelve hundred degree threshold."

She started to argue, "Enforcer's armor is no..."

I held a hand up. "I can do it. This is experimental armor, nothing like the standard issue. I can get in there before your Pyre-Suits get here. As you said, every second counts."

I looked at the fire crew start to work, some spraying water or firing oxygen inhibitor or foam grenades to try to starve the fire, while others with magic started slinging waves of super-chilled frost into the middle of the visible flames. They were a well-oiled machine.

The woman made a huffing sound in her throat then looked at me. "A charge weighs almost three hundred pounds, you're..."

I nodded, hearing the unspoken 'human'. "I can handle it." Even without my armor, I could probably drag it into place, I was a little stronger, a little faster than normal humans. But my armor, like my old standard-issue armor, had servos built in to make me as strong as many of the other races on the world. "Just tell me what to do."

I lowered my visor and almost coughed when I breathed in the smoke again, I let her see the determination in my eyes. Then she nodded once and paused when an announcement came out over coms that Queen Titania of the Summer Court was sending some of her people down to help mitigate the fire.

Fire was the domain of the Summer Court, just as ice was the domain of the Winter Court. The Greater Fae of her court could likely contain the fire ten times better than the containment crews here could.

All the crews seemed to relax a little at the news. At least this thing would be contained for sure before the forest caught if the Seelie were coming. They usually stayed well clear of anything on the world that didn't affect them directly, so I wonder why they were coming to our aid this time.

I listened intently to the fire marshal, who introduced herself as Hanalee, as she gave me instructions on where to place the charge. And once I activated it, I had sixty seconds to get clear. It didn't have a remote trigger, just in case a clump of stray cosmic radiation triggered it, so a timer it was.

The commander of the Alpha-Ring Brigade was approaching us, calling out my name, telling me to stand down. I said quickly to Hanalee, "Gotta get going. Be back in a flash." I grabbed the cryo-charge, hesitated, and with the aid of my armor's servos, went jogging straight into the fire before the angry-looking elvish commander could reach me.

Ok, not my most well thought out plan. Even in this new armor, I could feel the heat seeping in, but it wasn't anything I couldn't take. I slowed after a few steps and furrowed my brow as the flames seemed to move around me but not hit the armor.

Graz said, "This isn't the time to lock up, Shade."

And Mother prompted me, "Knith?"

I said, "Look at this..." I reached into the flames and the swirling chaos seemed to part to flow around my arm instead of engulfing it. "It's acting like... no..."

Mother sounded curious when she prompted, "Like what?"

It sounded silly but I shrugged and said, "Like magic. You know how it has a problem sticking to me."

Graz said, "Well you saw it with your own eyes earlier, did you see any glow?" They were two of the four people who knew I could feel and see magic.

I shook my head. "The fire was so bright, I wouldn't have noticed. But this..." I stepped into a gout of flame and it swirled out of my way. "Isn't natural."

Mother voiced my concern. "A spell? Sabotage?"

I shook my head then plodded forward, following the flashing coordinates on the map, the center of the blaze... and it was moving. "Nobody would be that foolish, they'd have to know it would be found out that the fire was intentional, and the punishment for sabotage of the world is spacing to suck hard vacuum."

I didn't have time to ponder it as the center of the fire was again moving up against the Bulkhead A wall. I lugged the drum-like charge along, my armor compensating for my uneven footing, keeping me upright as I slogged across ceramic deck plates that were glowing red hot.

How was it moving?

I asked, "Mother, I know the techs have been playing around with adapting Magic Resonance Scan tech into Brigade armor..."

"On it... it is not as precise as a dedicated unit but. Hmm... curious."

It still unnerved me a little how... alive she sounded to me. I've surmised that she had become self-aware in the thousands of years the Leviathan has been flying through space to our destination, but she is afraid to let anyone know, especially the Greater Fae who could switch her off at a moment's notice and have her reset to default settings, making her just a run of the mill AI again.

I prompted, "Care to share with the class? It's getting uncomfortably warm in here."

Graz made an unzipping motion then offered, "Are you crazy? This feels great in here, like a Fae hothouse."

I flicked my eyes toward her and she scrunched her head to her shoulders like she was afraid any sudden movement would set me off as she rezipped her lips.

Static filled com traffic assaulted my ears. Someone was yelling at me it seems. I'm sure it was the commander. What could be messing with coms? The channels are boosted by journeyman lesser Fae, we could fly through the residual radiation belts from an ancient supernova and still have coms. Wait... I could still communicate with Mother just fine. Was the minx purposefully introducing static?

"While the fringes of this tsunami of flame is physical fire, the core here seems to be violent eddies of compressed magic causing extreme heat," Mother said.

While I nodded at the confirmation to my hunch, Graz blurted, "Someone is doing this on purpose?"

The fire marshal's voice crackled in my ear, "Shade, do you copy? Our scanners aren't tracking you in there, there's some sort of magic interference. The epicenter is moving. Do you read?"

"I copy Hanalee. The fire is magic in nature, but I think there's more to it. Moving into position, ETA to heart, fifteen seconds."

After a moment's hesitation, she responded, "Magic? This was intentional?" She seemed to refocus and said, "First priority is to stop this before we have structural collapse, we can sort out the who's and why's later." Then she whispered, "Mother says three Greater Fae from the Summer Court are two minutes out, I'd prefer to get this contained before they get involved."

"On it. Shade out."

Ok, I was smirking a bit at that, so it wasn't just me who felt that if the Greater Fae had to pull our asses out of the literal fire, it would just reinforce the fact that without them, we'd all have perished long ago. It seemed the other preternatural races felt the same.

I stepped through a melted section of the bulkhead and moved into what looked to be someone's housing quarters, but everything was charred, the deck plates were melted in spots and the alloys of the walls were sagging... all the belongings were charred rubble. I moved through three walls that had almost perfectly circular holes burned through them. Like something had been burrowing through them.

The closer I got to the heart of the fire, the more I could taste magic like it was coating my tongue, and I could feel it moving. I stepped into a mechanical equipment room that looked to have something to do with environmental controls for this section, judging by the huge ducts and pipes that were melted through. In a clear path.

I could hear something over the roaring, magic-induced flames, almost like a whimpering. According to the map in my peripheral, we were almost against Bulkhead A again. Mother's readings showed the superstructure was reaching critical temperatures again. In that area there was no buffer between the forest and the bulkhead if the fire made it through, the forest was sure to go up like kindling.

Something huge was sort of flowing and squirming like it was curling itself up into a ball as it nestled against the wall. My jaw hung open when I realized what I was looking at. It couldn't be... so this is why the fire was acting like it was alive. It was some sort of huge creature with hyper-compressed magic radiating from it. And judging by the sounds, and the way it was curling up, it was afraid.

I said into coms as I set the cryo-charge down to move in for a closer look, "Han, we've got a little problem. I won't be able to set off the charge. There's something alive in here, I think it is causing all of this."

"We don't have a choice, the fire is about to breach the bulkhead, set the charge and get out. The higher-ups can examine the body later."

"Gods be damned woman. Whatever it is it is afraid. Just give me a minute to see if I can talk with it. If not then I'll set off the fleeking charge."

She started to argue but Mother anticipated me and cut the com channel. I inhaled and held my breath as I steeled myself. I started forward cautiously, calling out, "Hello? I'm Knith Shade, Brigade Enforcer. I'm not going to hurt you."

The ball of flame was huge, at least nine feet tall, it seemed to uncoil slightly.

I kept talking. "I know you're afraid, but I can help."

It unfurled more and backed away, flowing like a river of flame.

"It's ok. I won't hurt you."

It swung toward me and I almost tripped as I backpedaled, then I froze when the fire... blinked. I pulled back slightly to look at the saucer-sized eye, and I smiled as I made out a big muzzle. It was some sort of animal. "It's ok. Can you move over this way more? I know you don't mean to, but you're endangering everyone on the world. We need to move away from the wall."

I felt like a fool when I held a hand up for it to sniff like it were a canine, or fairy. Huge nostrils flared and it moved along with me as I backed away from the bulkhead. I noticed the flames were dying in fury and I didn't feel the heat radiating as much. "That's it. See? I'm not going to hurt you. That's a good..." Girl, boy? "...fire being."

It flowed like a snake with me and I chanced to step up to it when we were clear of the bulkhead and I realized in a flash of insight what I was looking at and the impossibility of it had me blinking. It couldn't be. Even among the Fae, it was just folklore. The Vikings had stories... and in all those legends, they were all female.

I reached up and placed a hand on its muzzle and scritched as I said, "That's it, good girl."

The Firewyrm closed her eyes and made a satisfied moaning sound. I grinned and patted her more enthusiastically. A Firewrym? By all the celestial gods, they were real? The power flowing off of her was diminishing and the flames settled into fluffy feather-like layered fur as she almost knocked me over when she nuzzled me.

I chuckled as I glanced around to see the fire slowly dying without her fear-fueled magic feeding it. Now that I could see her, I noted how much she looked like a combination of the legless dragons from old earth legends from a cultural division they called countries which they designated China, and the European division dragons.

Magic, had a problem sticking to me, and even Mab's mark needed her to renew it from time to time or it lost its hold. I took a chance, and with a thought I had my armor retract one of my gauntlets, exposing my hand.

Mother made a distressed sound as she gasped, "Knith!"

The air was almost painfully hot, but it had dropped from over a thousand degrees to around a hundred and twenty-five since the Firewyrm started to calm down, I think most of the heat was from the residual fire and superheated ceramic and metal around us.

Then I placed my hand on the beast, sinking my hand into the surprisingly soft fur. It practically purred as I placed my helmet against its massive head. "There we go sweetie, everything is going to be ok. I promise."

My head was filled with flashes of emotion, mostly fear and

confusion, and impressions of words, like 'door' and 'big dark' or 'afraid' and 'hide', 'lost' and 'home'. It was sentient, but like a small child. I withdrew my other gauntlet and my visor rose. I breathed in the smoke-filled scalding air, and hugged her head, whispering to her, "It's ok, baby girl. I've got you. You don't need to be afraid."

The Firewrym cooed and snuggled its massive head against me, and I smiled at the impressions I was getting from her. Was this how she communicated? I stroked her fur and reactivated my coms as I said while Graz timidly flew out of my helmet to hover in front of the beast's eye, waving from her hip. As she asked in a stunned voice, "Umm... Knith? Do you know what this is?"

I nodded and provided, "A Firewyrm, and if I'm right, just a baby."

Then I was on coms. "Hanalee, this is Shade. Situation is under control. You should make short work of the fire now. I need everyone to stay back until we can get someone in here who is good with young people. I've got a Firewyrm in here and she is frightened."

There was a long pause before a disbelieving Minotaur asked, "A... Firewyrm? But those are just... are you sure?"

I nodded to myself as I continued to scritch the thirty-foot long baby. "Pretty positive, she's actually pretty cute, but any stress will likely start this whole mess all over." Then I added... "I umm... I think she's Fae. We're sort of communicating."

Another pause and she started to speak, then instead blurted in an almost whisper, "Fuck me, you've got incoming."

Incoming?

I could feel the overwhelming magic approaching through the dwindling fires and knew who it was before the woman stepped through the flames as if she didn't feel them, gouts of swirling flame and heat flowing into her like she was absorbing the inferno as she walked up to us.

I moved my body between her and the Firewyrm, like that would do any good. Queen Titania hesitated when she saw me and with a sneer on her inhumanly beautiful face she hissed out, "You! I should have known. Every travesty has your mark on it."

I said in a wavering voice, knowing magic resistance or not, she could crush me with but a thought, just like Mab, "Leave her alone. She didn't mean to do this. She's..."

I trailed off when Titania just brushed past me to wrap her arms around the neck of the beastie and said, "It's ok, Ember, mommy's here."

This Ember seemed to undulate in excitement. I started to smile then froze when the Summer Lady turned to me, her hands bursting into flames as she spoke to Ember, "If she's hurt you..."

I held my hands up. "I'd never hurt her. She's a sweetheart! We're buddies."

She seemed to blink in shock when Ember gave me a big wet sloppy slurp with her immense tongue, leaving my entire face sopping wet. Eww. I scratched her under her massive jaw.

The woman studied me as Graz flew back into my helmet and burrowed down as far as she could get into my armor. She was terrified. Titania exhaled and said, "I'm done with you for now. Leave us, I need to get Ember back to her pen."

My armor barely sealed up in time as a fireball struck my chest, sending me flying back through all the holes in the walls pushing me until it made a ninety-degree turn and sent me tumbling across the deck back out in the open Ring. I came to a rolling stop at the feet of Hanalee and an overly miffed looking Brigade Commander. My visor slid up and I groaned, "Ow." Then I held up a finger before either of them could lay into me. "Queen Titania has things from here. I'm just going to lay here a minute and count my bruises."

Mother, in all her sarcastic glory, started playing Bad Reputation by a singer named Joan Jett, in my head. Every part of me ached too much to flip off the nearest observation camera. She chuckled at the thought, making me nervous about the neural interface of my experimental helmet again.

CHAPTER 3
Heavily Broken

It was an almost painful debriefing after the other two Fae of the Summer Court corralled all the fire into one spot instead of absorbing it as Titania had, and a cryo-charge snuffed it out. When crews went in to locate the Summer Lady, she was nowhere to be found. Nor I noted to myself, was the Firewyrm.

Engineers from every ring were showing up to assess the damage and Mother seemed distracted as she ran extensive system diagnostics and structural scans of every micron of the ring and its superstructure to assess the extent of the damage to her critical systems like life support.

The entire ring was shrouded in hazy smoke as the air scrubbers kicked into overtime to try to clean the air. Some scrubbers were damaged in the mechanical room Ember had hidden in so it may take weeks to clear the air.

Crews were out looking for all of the residents who were displaced to be sure of headcounts to verify there were no casualties.

And crews were looking to me for answers, seeing as how I was the only one to see the "supposed Firewyrm" besides the Summer Lady and she wasn't answering coms and Mother couldn't locate her anywhere on the world, they all ignored Graz's account, which made me angry. I hated how some races were discounted. And that wasn't just sour grapes being one of those races... well maybe.

While I was going over it for the fifth or sixth time, showing them footage from the various cameras on my armor to show I hadn't just gotten "disoriented" in the fire and was seeing things, word of Titania resurfacing came to us.

Commander J'mayaght's eyes were reading something in his heads up display, I could see the lights in his ice-blue eyes, his pointed ears twitching. He cursed in Elvish, "Ta'raght." Then he fixed me with his gaze. "Queen Titania and President Yang want us, your Commander Reise, and your partner in the FABLE office at Verd'real in thirty minutes. I swear, Shade if your reckless behavior puts me in a bad light in the Summer Court..."

I would have been a little excited to see the Summer Palace if I hadn't known I was about to have my ass handed to me. I was sort of persona non grata in the Summer Court since I sort of, well... after Titania's son tried to kill me and harvested my eggs, then tried to enthrall me with his glamour, I sort of arrested him. And after his trial I was also the one who operated the controls to carry out his sentence of being spaced... his body ejected out into the unforgiving hard vacuum of space.

So there was that.

While the elf was contacting his Enforcers to start canvassing the area to investigate where the Firewyrm had come from, I asked Mother, "Can you contact..."

She sighed with patience. "I've already sent word to Lieutenant Keller. And I took the liberty to access your Tac-Bike, I'm flying it here now, ETA ten minutes."

I grinned. "What would I do without you, Mother?"

She and Graz said at the same time, "Die."

Everybody is a comedian.

I'm sure my Grindle partner from the Fae and Brigade Liaison Enforcers office, or FABLE, was going to be wishing me a slow roast in one of the hells for getting him pulled into this. But that's what Dan and I had signed up for, being the bridge between the Fae and... well and everyone else living on the world.

Ok, neither of us signed up for it, we were assigned. The duplicitous Fae princess who, I think I might be dating... or something, was behind it along with Queen Mab.

Commander J'mayaght looked at me. "Lieutenant Shade, you're with me."

Mother sounded in my head. "Rerouting Tac-Bike now to A-Ring spoke terminal," as I stood at attention. "Sir!" Oh goody, a fifteen-minute ride with a superior who already didn't like me. Fun.

It was an awkward, silent ride in a Brigade personnel skimmer to the nearest spoke terminal then up-ring to the A-Ring. I had only seen Alpha-Stack's A-Ring in holos, waves, and pictures. The Beta-Stack A-Ring was the most awe-inspiring thing I had ever seen, except for seeing the Leviathan herself from space earlier that day, but the habitat ring of the Summer Lady? It was a world of its own.

Impossible lattices of flowering vines climbed the superstructure to hang from the girders supporting the day-lights far above, framing the view of the lower rings and the trunk in explosions of color. The forests were all flowering too, and every building and all the bulkheads were covered in moss and vines and flowers as well, the air was heavy with the sweet perfume from them which almost made me light-headed.

This would be what I would imagine one of the Old Earth religions would refer to as the Garden of Eden. And like that cautionary tale, I knew there were snakes and forbidden apples here too. Everything the Greater Fae did was deceptive.

Because they were all cursed with a powerful gaes, and literally could not tell a lie, they were the greatest of deceivers using the truth to lull you into complacency. And before you knew it, you'd find yourself and your descendants owing a debt to them and not quite understanding how they had tricked you into it.

Where the Winter Court saw it as a game and was cruel about the game most of the time, the Summer Court, in my opinion, was worse, since they did it with smiles and kindness for the most part, unless you run afoul of them as I did, then they can be even more cruel than the Winter.

We skimmed above the roads that were sculpted to resemble cobblestones once we dipped down from the spoke terminal to be swallowed in the thick canopy of impossibly huge trees which reached for the Day Lights over a mile above, which were off for the night.

I still find it hard to believe that each of the four A-Rings has almost two thousand square miles of space, four times that of the crowded C-Rings I had lived in prior to getting entangled with the Fae. Even more than the surface of the seven-mile diameter asteroid encased in the Heart sphere located... well located in the heart of the Leviathan. The workers and ore extractors there have virtually no gravity, so they can't even come farther out than the small D-Rings without requiring exoskeleton support or magic buffs to support their brittle bone structure in the higher gravity of the spinning rings.

We slowly elevated over the lower level traffic as we got clearance to fly in the priority lanes just above the canopy. My breath caught as we cleared the trees again as we flew along and the Summer Palace of Verd'real rotated into view, dominating the horizon as we sped toward it.

The Winter Court's Ha'real was in tune with the nature around it, looking majestic and... well, cold. Having a central pointed tower of opalescent white that stretched almost a half-mile high, with other lesser spires surrounding it, extending half that height, melding in with the bulkhead on one side and stretching out to the lake in the middle of the ring. Low structures were arranged at the base to create a walled courtyard of green that ran the whole length of the palace, and waterfalls fell into the courtyard from big jagged rocks that melded into the bulkhead beside the towers there.

But the Summer Court's palace? It 'was' nature. It looked to have grown out of the forest, covered in trees and moss and ivy, spires that looked to be made of impossibly huge tree trunks spiraling around each other reached over a half-mile high. The bulkheads were impossible to distinguish from the living wooden towers.

Colorful, large Fae birds flew in great flocks all around the palace, through the mist from a great waterfall that looked to be coming out of the walls of the ring itself, crashing down to blue shimmering lakes that completely surrounded the palace, preventing approach from the ground. I could spot hidden Elf and Fae lookouts and guards hidden all over in the canopy as we passed over.

If anything, I'd say that Verd'real was even more fortified, deceptively so than Ha'real.

Then I muttered as we approached a wall shimmering in my vision, "Oh shit. Graz, get against me!" Nobody else saw the massive dome of magic, the wards the Summer Lady had placed around her domain.

I heard her squeak as she burrowed down the front of my armor, "Not this again!" And the ship sank into the ward as we descended to the clearing of a courtyard below us.

Just like the Winter Palace, the power sparked off of my scatter armor, which would be useless against a spell of this magnitude anyway, and I felt the magic probing my body and mind.

As it probed, I pushed back, hard, growling at the foreign magics, "Get away from me!" As if it were alive, it recoiled, then it was gone and I was hissing out to the ward, "She's with me!"

Graz was spasming and glurking like she was being crushed by some invisible snake. The magic seemed to hiss back at me then abruptly released her.

This wasn't the first time I cursed the fact that even though she was a lesser Fae, her larger cousins actually did treat Sprites as vermin. So this ward and I were not destined to become friendly.

The others were looking at us as I pulled Graz out by the wings, held her in front of my face and asked, "You good?"

She shook her head as if to get the cobwebs out then almost pouted. "Yeah... I'm fine."

I let her go and she buzzed to my shoulder and we realized the commander and the pilot were looking at us like we had grown two more heads. They hadn't even noticed the wards. I explained, "Fae magic and I aren't on the best of terms. Titania's wards tried to... umm... prevent my and Graz's entry."

Then Commander J'mayaght blinked, realizing what had happened. "You mean to tell me the Queen's defenses tried to rebuff you?"

I nodded and carefully when Mother whispered in my head, "Careful."

I then responded, "Crush, us? Exterminate us? Yes."

The pilot said, "If the wards were up, you'd be paste. They're crafted by Queen Titania herself. And you're invited... the flying vermin, not so much."

Graz darted at the man, her dust sifting angrily, and I caught her wings and pulled her back to sit indignantly on my shoulder as she shouted at him, "You stupid big! You'll regret..." I made a zipping motion over her lips and she crossed her arms over her chest with a harrumph.

"As I said, I'm not on the best of terms with Fae magic." I pointed out.

The pilot looked at me like I were simple. "You'd be dead."

But the commander studied me then said thoughtfully, "Your scatter armor was sparking."

I nodded. "Exactly, it is what saved me my first time to Ha'real too." Lies, lies, all lies. But both Mother and Princess Aurora think it would be unwise for more people to know that I am partially immune to magic than absolutely have to. The two men looked at me suspiciously but said nothing else about it.

The commander and I were met by a dozen armed guards with magic focusing lances pointed our way when we stepped out. The Greater Fae of the Summer Court, had healthy bronze or ebony skin, whereas the Winter Court had skin so pale it bordered on snow-white but was equally alluring in its own way. And the members of both courts were equally and stunningly beautiful to the one.

It was explained to me in school, that Earth's star, Sol, beat down intensely on the Summerlands, and that healthy bronze of their skin was called a tan. And Sol did not favor the Winterlands so they became much paler than the other Fae.

The commander started to protest but a lance an inch from his eye dissuaded him of it, the guard wielding it, a very pretty and muscular Fae growled out a command, "Come out now, Winter!"

The pilot stepped out nervously, hands held up to show he was unarmed. The Guard craned his neck. "Who else is in there?"

The poor man looked ready to run at any moment as he swallowed and said, "Nobody."

The Guard motioned for him to step aside and three guards ran into the transport, then stepped back out a few seconds later, a female with gorgeous tattoos of glowing magic runes on her face, whispered to him. He looked at us and accused, "The alarm spells were triggered. Winter magic was detected."

I'm sure I looked as sheepish as I felt as I pointed at my crystal ice lips. "I have Mab's mark. And Graz here is from the Winter Court."

He jabbed his lance toward me as he leaned in. I had had about enough of that. I slapped away the blade of the lance and took a half step forward. "Get that out of my face. I'm Lieutenant Shade of the FABLE office, and I can bind you by law for threatening us, especially since we were invited by Queen Titania and President Yang themselves. Now lower your weapons or I'll shove them where the sun doesn't shine."

The man actually growled at me. "I am the Captain of the Verd'real home guard, you wouldn't dare, and wouldn't get a single step before I ran you..."

I took a single step forward as the commander was trying to call me off. I caught the shaft of the lance as the Fae instinctively swung it to defend. It was all I could do to catch it. His strength was many times mine but my speed was honed by years sparring with races faster than me and by my unique genetic makeup. I took his moment of shock, that a human was fast enough to block him, to pull a mag-band from a belt pack.

As I was saying, "Captain Yar, I bind you by law for assaulting a..."

The commander was snapping at me, "Shade... stand down! That's an order."

I sighed and then leaned in to look the Fae in the eye, something I'd never have done before learning more about Fae glamour, knowing they couldn't glamour you without your permission or they could face dire consequences with their own courts. I was showing him I wasn't afraid. I smirked and stepped back.

The man studied me as he lowered his lance and had the others do the same with a hand motion. "You know who I am?"

"What kind of liaison officer would I be if I didn't have files on all the high ranking Fae?"

This was just a repeat of the posturing that went on at Ha'real. Were Fae really this predictable? It was like everything was a test, a dick-measuring contest, only I didn't wish to play.

He asked with a smirk of his own, "Did you know that Shade means..."

I waved him off. "Nobody... yes."

He nodded, apparently done with me as he turned to the

commander. "Commander Reise, your pilot will have to stay with the vessel."

The Elf cleared his throat. "I'm Commander J'mayaght, I'm ranking officer of the Alpha-Stack and..."

Yar finished for him, "Your rank means nothing in Verd'real. This is the Summer Lady's domain."

Ahh... so the commander had invited himself along, trying to gain the favor of Titania. He wasn't requested, only my commander, my partner, and me. I realized that everyone attending were the ones that knew most of my capabilities, including the President. Only Titania herself wasn't aware of my little idiosyncrasies... or was she?

The Captain stood to one side. "Lieutenant, the Queen is expecting you. You'll have to leave your pet here."

Before I could blink, Graz shot off in an angry red blur, and the Captain froze. The Sprite buzzed in front of his face, her tiny sword a hair's width from his left eye. "Apologize, you dumb big, or we're all going to see just what's inside a Greater Fae's eyeball. Maybe all the stupid you've got in your head will fall out."

The man didn't even blink, he just stepped back a step and then bowed slightly. "It takes a rare gift to take me by surprise, noble Sprite. You've a warrior's spirit and your speed is formidable."

Hey! I had just done the same thing and Graz gets the recognition? Then again, humans were below all Fae, even lesser Fae, in the Greater Fae's eyes.

Graz was grumbling as she buzzed backward to my shoulder, "Damn straight. The day a big can..." I cocked an eyebrow at her and she quickly zipped her lips.

I sighed in resignation saying, "Her sorry little ass is with me."

The man grudgingly bowed to us and made an ushering motion as other guards blocked the commander. As we stepped past, Graz quickly unzipped her lips and whispered to the man, "She's got a weird fascination with my ass. It's a human thing." Then she zipped up again and threw away the imaginary key as I huffed in exasperation.

The man paced us as we walked up the steps to the doors that looked to be made of carved ivory, and I could see sigils and runes woven intricately through the structure like little filaments of silver gifting the impossibly delicate-looking construct strength and power. The Queens of the Seelie and Unseelie Courts were terrifying, the sheer amount of power they wielded and how they could even weave spells as complex as what I was seeing with but a thought.

I mentally questioned how much of this I was seeing with my innate ability and how much Mother was providing me from the residual magic scans of my armor's systems. She caught the thought and provided, "About equal parts." I poked her mentally to get out of my thoughts. I swear I heard a ghostly giggle.

Ever since I learned that many of the things I did, which I had always attributed to my armor, were actually just me. Like dissipating spells, I thought my scatter armor was doing or seeing some types of magic. It was like I was having to re-learn everything I believed about doing my job as Enforcer. I think in some ways I had been better off not knowing, then I wouldn't always be second-guessing the magitech of my gear.

The four guards at the doors stood at attention, and the Captain spoke a word of power and the doors swung inward, making no sound, not even a whisper of air as those massive doors moved through it.

He made an ushering motion and I swallowed and stepped inside, looking back to watch the doors swing silently closed on their ghostly wings. The captain wasn't coming with me? I started to turn as I wondered how I was supposed to find... ah.

Standing before me was the seven-foot wall of furry muscle of a Grindle. The ethereal lights above glinted off of his tusks, and his small, dark eyes were narrowed. Ok, my sort-of partner wasn't a happy camper. And how had he gotten here before me, and in dress uniform no less?

The only way he could possibly get here from the Beta-Stack before me... I paled. I wasn't a fan of Jump Pods. They felt like glorified translucent coffins to me. Spit out of one ring to free float in space to the jump terminal in another ring, with only a clear tube with the compressed gas thrusters at the top and bottom of it for micro-adjustments of your trajectory between you and the unforgiving hard vacuum of space.

Sure the clear plastic pods were spelled against micrometeoroid strikes, but there was so much that could go wrong. Well fine, maybe it was my own paranoia. I've only heard of two incidents in my life on the world. But both prospects were not on my things-to-do list. One had to be recovered by Ready Squadron at the very extreme limit of their range, and one is forever floating in space somewhere. It couldn't be located after it missed the jump terminal on the receiving end.

Jumping from ring to ring in the same stack was one thing, but Keller had to have done a lateral transit jump from one stack to a counter-rotating stack to get here first. And that is where it was as much number-crunching as grabbing your bootstraps and praying. Mother started to explain in my head, "It is one of the safest ways to travel, Knith. I can explain the math to..."

I muttered, "Nobody asked you, Mother."

Causing Daniel to blink at me in confusion. At least it got the grim look off his face. I pointed at my head. "Mother is nattering at me."

She harrumphed in my head.

He huffed then asked, "What shitstorm are you dragging me into now, Shade?"

"Is that any way to speak to your superior officer?"

"Let's see how superior you are with my hoof jammed down your throat."

"Promises, promises," I smirked.

He exhaled then smirked back. He was a good egg.

Graz asked, "Want I should make some bacon jokes for you, Kni... eeep!"

Daniel had snatched Graz from my shoulder, holding her by pinched wings right up to his face, and he huffed, sending her dust streaming as he growled, "Nobody was asking you, you freeloading thief."

Graz dangled there a moment, shrugged, then kissed him right on his wide nose. The big man exhaled loudly then chastised her as he dropped her, "Keep your yap shut in there, this isn't your court, and there's no telling what the Summer Lady may do to you if you mouth off."

She buzzed up to hide in my hair behind my ear before she fell half her body length.

Ok, so why did he intimidate her when I couldn't even get her to move out of my bedside table with her family?

He looked at me expectantly, apparently still wanting an answer from me when the doors opened again, and the Brigade Commander of our Beta-Stack stepped in... in his dress uniform as well. I looked down at my armor, feeling underdressed.

Commander Reise looked at me, ignoring Dan. "I swear to the gods, Shade if you've made the Brigade look bad."

I defended as I contemplated why everyone was assuming I did something wrong. "All I did was help out with the fire. I don't know why we're all being called in."

Then someone cleared their throat, we looked to the six armed guards who had been standing there while I bantered with Keller. They all looked perturbed. "If you down-ringers are done, the Queen awaits. Nobody keeps the Summer Lady waiting."

The guards seemed to form up around us. Not menacing at all... so we decided that maybe it would be prudent to follow as they started herding us forward. I thought I caught Graz muttering something about Summer tin soldiers. She was going to get us all adorning Titania's gardens with roots and leaves, wasn't she?

I've often wondered about the animosity and rivalry of the two courts, and what had spawned it. But all of the history files and even old physical paper books I've found didn't lend any clarity on the subject. I had asked Graz once and she just said, "Summer sucks." And when I asked Mac, he was cryptic as always. "Things often do not follow logic when it comes to matters of the heart."

I assume he means when King Oberon, who I still think he is, had married Queen Mab, but then cheated on her later with the Summer Lady. But that didn't track, because it is said that Oberon had married the Winter Lady to stop the hostilities and the Winter Court's decline into violence.

I felt as if my neck was on a swivel as I took everything in. The palace was as beautiful on the inside as the outside, only instead of looking to be made of trees and wood, the inside seemed to be carved from one solid block of ivory. Sweeping ceilings and grand staircases were everywhere the eye looked. Even the grand chandeliers were seamless as if they grew out of the ceiling and there didn't seem to be a source for the light they shed.

We were led through some doors into what looked to be a greenhouse carved from a single, impossibly clear crystal. And in it, was a frightening receiving hall. It was lined by an orchard of trees. The trunks of which looked to be formed like beautiful men and women of all races, their arms reaching up to the light, becoming branches with large green leaves and flowers blooming.

I would have looked at the trees in awe if I hadn't known what they were. They were the people who had displeased the Summer Lady in some way. Where the Winter Queen had a habit of transforming those who had slighted her into ice statues, the Summer Queen felt it appropriate to punish people by changing them into living trees.

Maybe for a day, week or month, and in some cases, centuries or more. Some, she vowed, would adorn her halls and bedchambers until the Leviathan reached our destination in another five thousand years.

I was chanting in my head, "Don't piss off the Queen. Don't piss off the Queen." as we moved up to the raised throne of moss and flowers on a platform that dominated the far end of the space. Fairies and other tiny Fae flitted about, pollinating the flowers in the room, leaving twinkling trails of light.

One tree caught my eye, a female centaur rearing on her hind legs. Ah, so that's why they said the prior Commander of the Alpha-Stack had retired two decades ago. She was a gorgeous tree with a fierce, defiant look on her face, and white blooming flowers on her branches.

I almost jumped out of my skin when the Summer Lady whispered in my ear, "Beautiful, isn't she? I can't wait until you adorn my palace... what sort of blooms might you produce?" I stumbled back. She had just been sitting on her throne a moment before, with the President looking longingly at her.

My mouth worked without sound in my shock. She grasped my chin and turned my head side to side, examining the ice of my lips. Her Fae strength made resisting futile. She furrowed her brow then quickly leaned in and actually licked my lips. The warmth of her tongue sent a pleasant, involuntary shiver through me as she released my chin and contemplated for a moment before saying, "You wear Mab's mark. Perhaps you'll adorn her halls as a sculpture instead." She sounded bitter about my ice lips.

I almost apologized for some reason but she wasn't there. I spun, looking around to see she was back on her throne. I've never seen speed like that, even in a Greater Fae, so it had to be magic.

She spoke as we arrived and her guards formed a ring around us, "Now that we are all here, President Yang..."

"Kyoto, please, majesty." The very married president, her half-elven features making her look elegant and seductive, was fawning over the Summer Lady just as much as she does the Winter Lady. She had never met either, even as president, until the events that led up to me being assigned to form the FABLE office.

It was almost embarrassing that our leader was a Fae fangirl, and I wanted to grab her and shake her to tell her to snap out of it and act as a President should. The Summer Lady was eating up the adoration though as she gave a dazzling smile to the half-elf that had even me warming up in some inappropriate places. "Of course, Kyoto, dear."

Oh, don't feed the monster, Titania. I'm sure the President had almost orgasmed on the spot at the Summer Lady calling her dear. I cleared my throat, causing... Kyoto to look toward me. She saw my expectant look, then she stood taller, straightened the hem of her blouse and the fire and steel that won her the election reasserted itself as she stood tall and proud.

Better.

Titania looked perturbed, like I had taken a toy away from her, then continued, "I wished to address the... unfortunate events of this evening."

I prompted, "You mean the frightened Firewyrm who had inadvertently burned her way through B-Ring and threatened the forest?"

Yang shot me a scathing look as Riese muttered, "Shade, stand down."

Titania said from beside me as she was now walking around me, studying me again, "No, it is alright, I admire her directness." Then she asked me, "But aren't Firewyrms just legend?"

I could feel light playful magics that felt like a gentle embrace and smelled of all things green as it gently cajoled me. I slapped it away in my mind and she blinked in surprise then smiled widely, it was as frightening as it was beautiful. She dragged a finger along my shoulders as she passed behind me, giggling out, "So what the boy was prattling on about you is true..." Boy? What boy? Was she referring to my resistance to magic?

She stopped in front of me and locked eyes with me, and I could see the flame where her pupils should be. And she was gone, speaking from her throne again. "Yes... a Firewyrm. My Firewyrm."

Commander Reise spoke up, "Where might we find this... Firewyrm?" He sounded disbelieving, then added, "your Highness? It caused a lot of damage, and we are still trying to locate all of the residents of the area to ensure there were no casualties besides those sent to medical with burns and smoke inhalation. And we'll need to know who released it into..."

She waved him off. "Of course. That is why all of you are here right now. I wish for you to arrest the only person it could possibly be. It would do her good to work down in the mines in the Heart."

Then she warned, "But no, I will not tell you where Ember is. Nobody will touch her, nor will her existence be disclosed to anyone who hasn't heard Lieutenant Shade prattle on about it."

He started to say, "It put not just the citizens of Alpha-B at risk, but..." as I took a step forward to be even with him and I offered, "It's got the mind of a child. She was lost and afraid and didn't mean any harm."

Queen Titania cocked an eyebrow as Reise chastised me, "How would you..."

I crossed my arms, realizing only after I did it how petulant it probably looked as I blurted, "Because she spoke with me... or sort of gave me impressions of... well she communicated her fear, and something about the 'big black', it was all jumbled."

Now the Summer Lady looked positively shocked as she told him while she seemed to study me with interest, like this was the first time she had seen me, "She is right. Firewyrms are lesser Fae, sentient, not animals. They mature slowly, and Ember is just over five thousand years old. With the physical and mental capacity of a three-year-old. They mature in a couple hundred thousand years."

President Yang spoke carefully, her brow pinched, "But the charter specifically banned any fire nature elementals, Fae, or other preternatural from joining the population of the Worldship, as fire is the most dangerous thing on a space vessel."

I didn't know of such a ban. I was under the impression that Queen Mab had basically tricked the Humans of Old Earth into giving seats to every single Fae and member of the preternatural races. I wracked my brains trying to think of what races in legends were not part of the population on the world. All that came to mind were Firewyrms, dragons, and demons. But even the Fae say that demons are just fairy tales.

Could it be true that there were dragons on Earth that were left behind? I mean, if there really are Norse Firewyrms... And

Firewyrms were Fae? If dragons existed, were they Fae too? I had so many questions for Aurora when we had lunch tomorrow. The only question was, what were the answers going to cost me? Even though I think we're dating-ish, not even she gives information up freely. It is just the nature of the Fae.

The President blinked in shock as she asked, hurt, "You... you broke the contract?"

The Queen looked mad that anyone would accuse her of that, even if it were true, but she schooled her face and then nodded and said with emotion in her tone, "I couldn't leave her... she's just a baby. I am willing to offer recompense to the Presidential Office for this minor oversight. Every elected president since Exodus has petitioned the Fae courts for offices in an A-Ring. And as I only hold dominion over the Alpha and Gamma-Stacks, as Winter holds the others, I am willing to grant Presidential offices and quarters in Gamma in recompense."

Yang's disappointment turned to one I was quite familiar with whenever politicians were given a political boon, a scheming smugness as she wondered how she could use this as leverage against her rivals. I could see her quick mind going through the possibilities. Ah... there was the president I voted for.

She inclined her head in acceptance, then I could see her eyes widen slightly when she obviously made the realization that she would be living among the people she idolized. Been there done that, I actually preferred the C-Ring since everyone in the A-Ring treated me like an outsider and I definitely didn't feel welcome there even though it was a necessity with me being forcibly assigned to FABLE.

Yang, on the other hand, was half-Elf, and that would afford her some respect, as the Elves were seen almost as equals in the estimation of the Fae. The prestige of being the first President invited to dwell among the Fae would give her more political clout than any of her predecessors.

I did note and tried to hide the smile threatening on my lips, that it was in the Gamma-Stack, not Alpha. The Queen was distancing the President as far away from her as she could while making it look like restitution for breaking the charter. I froze, realizing the Summer Lady was watching me piece it all together. She smirked then turned away.

Reise looked around then said, "We'll need to see where you are holding the Firewrym. How have you hidden it on the ship for so long? I just queried Mother and she can't find it on the ship's schematics and all her scans are coming up empty."

The Queen flicked her finger and the commander glurked, his mouth covered with leaves and vines. "I didn't bring you here to investigate. As I said, there is only one possible suspect as she is the only one who can lower the wards to let Ember escape. I want you to arrest Queen Mab."

Then she looked at me. "And all know that since you..." She looked down her arm and finger at me, "are her pet, you are bound to not arrest her. You wear her mark to assure you do not. That is why the Grindle is here too."

I growled, "I'm nobody's pet. And how can you be sure it was Mab?"

"This is tedious. As I have said, only she and I can drop the wards at the doors of Ember's pen. And since I know it was not me, then logic dictates the only possible answer. That it was the Winter Lady. Only she can visit my Ember without me, as I can her Flame."

I looked at the commander who was still trying to pull the leaves off his mouth and contemplated her words. The Greater Fae couldn't lie... so... "Wait... Flame? There's another Firewyrm on board?"

The Queen closed her eyes, looking to chastise herself for her slip, then she opened them and smiled innocently, to devastating effect. "Did I forget to mention that? Yes, Flame is Ember's older sister. Mab and I have been raising them."

I nodded as I wondered how Mother couldn't locate two flaming creatures who have been hiding somewhere on the world since the Leviathan was built. Maybe thermal... "I've tried thermal scans, and structural resonance scans, there is just no place on my schematics where a Firewyrm could be. I cannot scan the Palaces though."

That was a thought. Instead of complaining about Mother listening in on my thoughts through the neural interface of my armor again, I decided to ask point-blank to see if she denied it. "Are you hiding Ember in your palace? Where Mother isn't allowed to scan?"

The woman actually tittered. "You want information from me for free? I have already volunteered more than was needed to implicate Mab. I never thought she'd go that far. What do I get if we play your game?"

"The satisfaction of knowing you helped the people of the world instead of just sitting in your shiny palace looking down on us all?" I mirrored her sweet innocent smile with malice.

She chuckled at that as the President started to reprimand me but Titania raised a hand stalling her as she gave me a wicked grin. I almost backpedaled as the Queen was beside me in a blink, whispering in my ear. "Why shouldn't I look down upon you? You had my son spaced."

My body shivered, it was all I could do to stop from running away screaming. Instead, I turned my head to look her straight in the eye, knowing that she could enthrall me into a drooling mess of desire in an instant, but I wanted her to see the truth as I spoke low so the others couldn't hear, "I didn't do anything, HE brought it on himself by killing people, harvesting their organs." Then I hissed, "He harvested my eggs and tried to steal my will." Then I reined in my rage and whispered calmly, "That is why he was found guilty under the law and was spaced. Did I take pleasure in being the one to carry out the actual sentence?"

I narrowed my eyes and growled out louder, "Yes."

She chuckled from her throne. It was disconcerting when she

did that. I looked up at her as she said in contemplation, "I can see now why Mab keeps you around. You are... interesting, and not afraid of us."

Actually, I was terrified.

She continued, "Just for the way you spoke with me just now, I would normally have had you growing roots, and learning the folly of such impudence adorning my bedchambers as a tree. But since I can't fault you for my son's minor indiscretions, I find myself liking you."

Then she shrugged. "A deal then? I answer three questions for you, and you agree to run along with your partner to arrest the one responsible for releasing my dear Ember and causing this whole mess."

"Or how about you stop playing Fae games and... mmpf" Graz buzzed out of my helmet in distress as vines tied a handful of leaves in my mouth. I could actually taste the magic, they weren't real, it was a spell. I grabbed them and yanked them away, they couldn't grab hold of me and dissolved in my hand as I started to pull a mag-strip from my belt. "Queen Titania, I bind you by law for using magic against..."

President Yang snapped out, "Lieutenant Shade, stand down!"

The Summer Lady again put up a halting hand then cocked her head at me, nodding. "I see why you are so fascinating to Mab and Sindri now... and why that old doddering fool, Oberon, favors you. Even our magics cannot bind you for long." She had just been testing me? And the mention of her illegitimate son's name brought up an involuntary shiver. He... had made me a victim, and I feel perpetually broken because of it.

"Please, let us play. Deal?" she asked.

I told her, knowing I'd likely not even get three answers from her if I didn't, "You realize we'd arrest the one responsible whether we make this deal or not don't you? You should just be forthcoming with your answers."

She shrugged and I sighed, "Fine. Three answers, but only to questions I specify as part of the bargain. And not sealed with a..."

I felt as if I were on fire as power poured into me, singeing my very soul as the Summer Lady kissed me. My icy lips sizzling with steam. A tiny portion of me was aroused by the kiss and then she let go of me and I dropped to the ground gasping as she said, "Done. Sealed with a kiss." Then she said from her throne as she licked her lips, "Are you sure you aren't Fae? Your wording was quite specific."

She had the sort of incomprehensible world-building magic that Mab had, and I let Daniel help me to my feet as I swayed, my body trying to recover from so much magic being forced into me.

Graz said, "Umm... Knith?" as she stared at my lips.

Yang gasped.

I absently reached up and heard the familiar clink of my gauntlet on ice, then froze. I retracted the nano-panels from my fingers and touched again. My upper lip was still ice, but my lower lip... it burned like fire without singeing my skin. Fuck me sideways and space me naked, I had just been marked by another Fae Queen. Why?

She said smugly from her throne, "Couldn't allow Mab to be the only one to hold sway over you. So now ask your three questions, a contract is a contract after all."

I glared at her then slowly smiled. "No. Our investigation will uncover the truth anyway. But now, the Queen of the Summerlands owes me three answers. I'll hold onto those questions for some future time. And you get to simmer, knowing that you owe me."

As I started to turn to leave, she hissed, "Insolent Human, don't think you bested me!"

I felt sluggish as my lip flared, I looked at my feet and I was starting to grow roots. I pushed at the magic, growling at it as I started to feel stiff. "Get... off... of... me!" Titania gasped and I tore my foot from the ground, snapping roots.

My anger got the best of me, and I shouldn't have done it but I growled back at her, "Like a mere Human bested your son, a Greater Fae?" It was petty of me and I regretted it the moment it passed my lips.

She was incensed as she swung her hand to point at a tree beside the throne which was bearing flowers and fruit. "And he's paying for that failure now!"

My heart started to beat faster, the panic was rising in my chest as I blinked at the impossible. How had I not seen it earlier? The tree by the throne was reaching to the lights like the others, only one branch was but a stump. And I recognized the pretty man in the bark of the trunk, the sneer on his lips when he had been turned to wood so familiar. I took a step back stumbling to be caught by Dan.

It was Sindri.

My mouth worked soundlessly until I finally ground out hoarsely, "Sindri? But... but he was spaced. He was... convicted and... spaced. I did it myself." The world spun, not making any sense.

She was all smiles now as she said, "Yes, he was, and yes, you did. My son had made a deal with a Remnant captain from his cell during the trial. You spaced him, which is a cruel and unusual punishment for a Fae, as it does not kill us, our bodies just freeze and we float endlessly through space, aware and awake the whole time."

Shrugging she was suddenly standing at the tree caressing the cheek of the man I hated more than anything. "As it was, Sin floated out there for six hours until the Remnant wreck was able to retrieve his frozen body. He was brought before me and now he is paying the price for failure and for the sins he perpetrated on the world. I may keep him this way until we reach our destination. The foolish boy."

I looked from her at the leafy Sindri, to the President who was looking sheepish and then to the commander who was still gagged. He and Yang didn't look surprised. I tried to make any sense of the world, then grabbed a mag-band. "Restore him. I'm taking him into custody."

She shook her head and giggled. "You cannot. He was tried for his crimes already and was sentenced to spacing. You yourself carried out his sentence, did you not? Since the sentence was passed and executed, he cannot be tried a second time for the same crimes. It is the double jeopardy loophole in the laws which we all must abide."

I wanted nothing more than to slap the smug look from her pretty face, then chop down the wooden Sindri and use him as kindling. But President Yang was telling me with regret, "It is true, Knith. We didn't wish to upset you when we learned of this, but there is nothing to be done for it as they are following the letter of the law and not it's intent."

This was the first time I had witnessed that she didn't seem enamored with the Fae.

I just stumbled back again and heard myself saying, "I need to go. Need to think."

Titania said from where she now stood at the doors, "I expect you will be having your partner arresting Mab, post-haste."

I blinked at that, pushing aside the shock and... fear... that was eating at me and narrowed my eyes at her. Her outrage at her son's demise was all just an act. She had been playing me for a fool, having him right next to her throne-like that the whole time. I really hated the Greater Fae.

I ground out, "We will conduct a thorough investigation, and will bring the guilty party to justice as I promised. If when the investigation concludes that the Winter Lady was involved, only then will she be arrested."

I heard her chuckling as Keller paced me as we left the guards escorting us. I looked up at the man. "I need some time to process this. We can start the investigation in the morning." He just nodded as he studied me. Then I asked the air almost desperately, "Mother?"

"Tac-Bike ETA, thirty seconds." She replied quickly.

I nodded in thanks as Graz landed on my shoulder, looking sympathetic as Mother started playing a song, called Heavily Broken by a group named the Veronicas, in my head.

As usual, very apropos.

CHAPTER 4
Stray Cat Strut

I had a fitful sleep when I got home. I woke up with a headache, I rubbed my eyes as I sat up in bed, groaned out, "Oww... I really hate the Greater Fae."

A voice beside me in my bed said, "Really now? All Greater Fae?"

My eyes shot open and I looked over to see an overly amused, breathtaking woman sitting beside me, biting her lower lip to hold back a grin.

Aurora Ashryver, the Winter Maiden, Princess of the Winter Court, was perhaps the most beautiful creature I had ever laid eyes upon, with her doll-like features, flawless skin, flowing white and silver hair, with those sublime pointed ears sticking through her locks, were coupled with bright violet eyes which always had me gaping at her.

I shook my head as I heard Graz's muffled voice coming from my nightstand her family had commandeered as their home. "Really put your foot in it this time, Knith, you're dumb even for a big."

My eyes were locked on the amused princess in my bed, the left one twitching at the thought, as I said to the side like Rory couldn't hear me, "Shut up you flying rat."

Then to Aurora, I said, "That's not what I said."

Mother, ever so helpful, said in a tinny tone, "Negative, the voice records show that you did indeed..."

"Not helping!"

Then I shook my head at the woman who was smothering her smile with her delicate hand, with graceful fingers tipped with perfectly manicured nails of ice. "I'm just frustrated. Sorry, of course, there's at least one Greater Fae I really enjoy the company of."

She giggled and leaned in, our lips almost brushing. "Good. I'm fond of a particular human too." She pulled back, leaving me panting in want as she tapped my lips. "One who still tilts at windmills I see."

I squeaked out, "Not that I'm complaining... at all... but why are you in my bed, Rory?"

She gave me a quick peck on the lips then bounced off the bed and said, "I want pancakes. You were out hard when I arrived so I thought I'd sit and wait for you to wake."

"Again, not that I'm complaining, but weren't we having lunch, not breakfast? And how did you get past the door security? Wait, don't answer that, I really don't want to know."

She pouted, looking deceivingly innocent. "Our noble Sprite friend, Graz let me in, and do I need an ulterior motive to see you earlier than our lunch date? And if you'd rather me not sit in your bed..."

I sighed and grinned. "If you were anything but Fae, I'd say that no with a smile about ulterior motives. But seeing as how you are your mother's daughter then I'd have to reluctantly say yes. And is it a date? I've been trying to pin down what we are doing... I'm rather fond of, well, being around you."

"But not in bed?"

I sputtered out, "No, yes, I mean... oh just space me naked. I mean, I just want to define our relationship."

Someone, I think it was Graz or one of her significant others in their trinary coupling, called out, "Really smooth there, Knith."

My face was burning and I wanted to just smother myself with a pillow, then Mother chimed in helpfully, "I'm with the flying rat on... this... one..." Her voice becoming more emotionless and mechanical as she trailed off.

Rory cocked an eyebrow and looked at the closest camera in the room. "Come now Mother. This isn't the first time you slipped around me and emoted. Aren't we past this now? I'll not be disclosing your secret to anyone. I'm just amazed that it was Knith you chose to, come out to as it were. Though she does have that effect on people."

Mother responded in her tinny emotionless tone, "Please restate your query, original request not understood."

Rory looked at me and narrowed an eye. "Why did that sound like she was, what do you call it... when you extend your middle finger as you do frequently?"

Graz buzzed out of the hole in the nightstand and up in front of her, then landed on the extended finger the Greater Fae offered helpfully. "Flippin' the bird, flipping you off, the ol' one-finger salute, the universal..."

Rory chuckled at her as I sighed out, "She gets it, Graz. She was just baiting. It's what her people do. You of all people should know that."

The princess in my room said, "Fine, keep playing your games, Mother." Then she turned to me. "As for your questions, that isn't the way our game works, and you know it... I answered one question, now it is your turn. You can choose from, why do you wear the Summer Lady's mark? Why has the Summer Court cut off all communications with the Unseelie? Or, may I have another kiss?"

She smirked and I leaned in to kiss her, our lips barely brushing, then she grabbed a handful of my hair and pulled me into her, a sizzling sound accompanied by steam from Titania's mark boiling off the frost on her lips.

She released me and I felt light-headed, a goofy smile on my lips. Then she pointed at me when she realized what I did, answering the one question that gave her no information. I shrugged without apology. "My turn. As much as I'd like to think you were here just for an intimate encounter, why are you in my quarters so early?"

Her head tilted back and she laughed the silvery laugh that set off a tuning fork in my nether regions in the most pleasant of ways. "If I hadn't designed your genes myself, I'd swear you were Fae.

You play this game well."

Then she sighed and said, "After news of a fire in the Alpha-Stack spread through the world, I tried to contact you, but Mother informed me you were among the first responders, but wouldn't supply any additional information. Naughty AI. Then shortly after, the two courts stopped communications, and the Winter Lady has gone missing."

Shrugging she admitted, "I was worried when I didn't hear from you. And also curious if you could help shed some light on what is happening? In the absence of the Winter Lady, the Unseelie are looking to me for answers. I have none."

Before I could say anything she got a playfully mischievous look on her face as she said, "And I will volunteer another answer for free. I'd like to think of us as courting, even though it gives mother apoplexy that I've taken an interest in a human, of all suitors at hand."

Ok, my blush was threatening to be my end now as I felt bashful satisfaction that I hadn't been imagining that what we had together felt like dating, even though she had never admitted it before this.

I nodded and squeaked out, "Mother? Ship's time?"

"It is zero six-thirty. You have thirteen messages from Commander Reise, three from President Yang, and one from Queen Titania's representative to the FABLE office. Shall I play them?"

"No... thanks though. I'm not looking to adding to my headache until after I'm fully awake."

I looked at the imp I wished to ravish just then, then sighed and said, "Pancakes it is. Daniel and I start our investigation into this clusterfuck at eight. I'll have him meet me at Stacks down-ring in C. Until then, I'm all yours."

She chuckled and said, "There are places to eat here in the A-Ring you know, Knith."

I nodded but said, "Yeah, there are, but Stacks is our place."

Aurora's toothy smile was almost predatorily seductive. "We have a place? That pleases me."

I said to her and Graz, "Now shoo, let me get ready."

Rory chuckled as she carried our Sprite friend from my sleeping chamber. "Boooo."

Graz explained, "She's got a weird hangup about people seeing her naked. It's not like you don't have all the same stuff she does, and I've got two-thirds of it. I'll never understand humans." Then she whistled, and her family streaked out of the drawer like a drunken line of sparkling lights. I sometimes forget that the pollinator of a tri-sex species is the one in charge of their family since they are so rare.

I said as I slipped out of bed and took a quick sonic shower and shrugged into my armor as I called out the door, "Just a heads up, Rory. Every Enforcer of the Brigade is looking to arrest your mother."

That was met with silence for a few awkward seconds before she muttered, "Of course she's involved."

I stepped out into the room and Graz buzzed over to stand on my shoulder inside my helmet, hanging on to my ear to steady herself. She wasn't as graceful in the gravity of these upper rings, which made me wonder why she chooses to live with me up here.

Then I asked as I glared at the two royal guards standing by my entry door, "You ever ride on the back of a Tac-Bike?"

Her guards looked alarmed. "Highness..."

She held up a halting hand and just said, "Follow." Then to me, she added, "Sounds exciting."

I nodded and removed my helmet to hand to her. "You have no idea."

She was squealing in glee a minute later as we were blasting down the spoke toward the C-Ring and Irontown, my hometown here on the world. To the diner I first ate with Rory at, Stacks. I'm still not sure if the eatery is named that for the stacks of the ship, or for the stacks of pancakes that were the specialty there.

The wind in my hair was exhilarating, but Graz burrowing in my armor was uncomfortable. I'd have to get Aurora a helmet of her own if we're dating... or courting now. Mother fairy humper, I was dating the Winter Maiden. My smile was threatening to split my face as we emerged into morning traffic in the C-Ring.

Before long, we pulled up to Stacks, with Rory's security detail right behind us in her gleaming white manta ray shaped luxury sport skiff. She narrowed her eyes at them as she handed me my helmet back when we got off the bike and I mag-locked it. Her guards

looked put out and just stood by her skiff, looking all kinds of
conspicuous as they took aggressive guard stances. Yeah, way to
blend in.

I guess I was one to talk, stepping into the diner with a literal
princess on my arm. The hostess saw us coming and was already
shooing a family from the booth we have used in the past, ushering
them to another table.

She clopped up to us on her dainty hooves. "Princess Aurora,
Lieutenant Shade, your booth is available. Please have a seat, I'll
have your usual, two Stack Plates out post-haste."

Like many of us down-ringers, she was completely enamored
with the Greater Fae. They almost never ventured lower than the B-
Ring. And all we knew about them were from the documentaries on
the waves, what we were taught in school, and the glorified fairy
tales we were told as children.

Graz called out as she popped up in my collar, "And a
strawberry! The biggest you got."

I tapped her head with a finger, causing itchy dust to sift onto my
skin as I contradicted her, "Just a strawberry quarter. I don't want to
be depositing her at the drunk tank for disorderly behavior again this
week."

"Hey! That was just the one time, and I..."

"Graz?"

"Fine, you overbearing big."

Rory offered helpfully as we slid into our booth, both on the same side much to my pleasure, "You may partake of some of my syrup if you wish, noble Sprite." She gave me a defiant nose scrunch.

I whined, "You're not the one who'll have to put up with her hyperactive little ass all day... she..."

I trailed off as something on the wave screen above the stools at the counter. I tuned out Graz's complaint of, "Did you just call me little? And there's your obsession with my perfectly shaped butt again."

"Turn that up please?" I asked.

The hostess nudged her chin to the goblin busboy behind the counter, and he tapped the control and the volume on the news wave turned up. It was En'lein... Eileen Brightleaf, the gorgeous full-blood Wood Elf reporter for the news station LNN.

She was standing close to the fire-ravaged and melted bulkheads where Ember had been burrowing. The repair crews and Mother's automated repair drones were busy reinforcing sections and cutting the debris into more manageable sections to haul away before permanent repairs could begin.

Alpha-Stack Brigade Enforcers were standing at the barricades and crime scene tape that kept the lookie-loos from messing up any evidence or getting themselves hurt. Crime scene techs were scouring the area. I'd have to access all their findings as soon as I started the investigation with Keller.

Eileen was reporting that "It is still not known what started the raging inferno that could burn through ceramic and melt alloys that can withstand fractional C debris strikes. But rumors are circulating that the Winter Court is suspected, and the Enforcers tasked to the FABLE office are looking to detain Queen Mab herself for questioning by order of President Yang. Could this be the beginning of another great Fae War? We will keep you up to date as information is made available to us. This is Eileen Brightleaf, reporting for Leviathan Network News."

I was shocked that they were aware of the meeting with the President, for only a moment, before I saw Eileen smiling toward Commander J'mayaght who was behind the barricades overseeing his men.

Swell, the commander was butt hurt that he wasn't included in the meeting with Queen Titania and President Yang and that I and a commander from a different stack were. He was going to make my investigation as difficult as possible by leaking information to the press like this, wasn't he?

I just rubbed my temples, feeling my headache coming on again. At least he wasn't boneheaded enough to let slip that there was a Firewyrm on the world... that would cause a shipwide panic.

Rory asked, "Is everything ok, Knith? So they really are looking to detain mother."

I sighed and said, "Let's just have a peaceful breakfast before we have to get into all that unpleasantness, please?"

She nodded, studying me, then belying my own words, as I just stared at my first fork full of the sinfully light and fluffy pancakes and said with a raspy dry mouth, "Lord Sindri is alive and on the world."

She dropped her own fork in shock. Her half brother had been her rival and then he tried to kill me... I had stopped him, and my testimony and the evidence I had gathered in my investigation before he captured me was what had had him condemned. She never shared with me her feelings about that. I was just some random enforcer and he was her blood.

We never discussed it because, to tell you the truth, I still haven't fully recovered emotionally from it. As I said before, he made me a victim, and I'm nobody's victim. That incongruity had me second-guessing my every decision ever since then... I'm broken and I don't know how to fix myself, but Rory makes things better. She doesn't seem to look at me any differently, even though I do.

I stood and held a hand out to stop her from getting up. Graz looked up from where she sat on the table, a full quarter of a strawberry on her lap. "I just need some fresh air... I'll be right back." I pointed out front as another Tac-Bike pulled up. "There's Keller. He's early. Order him up a plate?"

Then I headed to the back hall, the restrooms, and the back door as I fought off the memory of what I had gone through with Sindri. Was this some sort of PTSD? As I stepped outside to breathe in the fresh air, an impossibly strong hand grabbed me and yanked me beside the door in the alley.

It barely registered to me that it was the Winter Lady in her 'Mable' human disguise before she was kissing me. She took great delight in my aggravation when she renewed her mark on me every few days this way, before the considerable power she puts into it, wears off because of my partial immunity to magic. She could simply just cast, likely from anywhere on the world, but she insists it be sealed with a kiss each time. I'm sure it was just that she enjoyed my consternation.

Again it felt like I was burning from the inside out, being destroyed and reborn as her magics seared my body and mind. She was putting more into me this time. I finally was able to push her off of me.

I gasped and pushed down the inappropriate tinge of arousal that always accompanied these random ambushes of hers. Why couldn't we just schedule a consistent time and place? "Mab! I mean, your highness. Are you aware that the Brigade is looking to detain you for questioning?" Then I took a chance, "Ember got out and Titania says you did it."

She smiled sadly and said, "That's why I had to do this, Lieutenant. It isn't personal, I just need time to find out what really happened."

I sighed, knowing I couldn't take her in myself, my partner would have to since I had an inadvertent binding Fae contract with her that I would not arrest her. It was never meant to be for perpetuity, but since it wasn't specifically worded that way, she uses the loophole like the Fae she is.

"What do you mean, why you had to do this? And that's my job to find out what happened."

She shrugged and stepped back, shimmering and I almost lost track of her, but I could sense her don't look here spells. And the alley door slammed open, Keller and two other Enforcers filed out with him. Their visors were down, scatter armor active, and Magic Mitigating Guns or MMGs drawn.

Keller said, "Queen Mab of the Unseelie Court, consider yourself bound by law. We need to bring you in for questioning for suspected arson in the Alpha-Stack B-Ring."

I turned to look at where Mab had walked off to under her spells. Could they see her still? That's when I felt the mag band being slapped on my wrist. I turned to look up at Keller, intending to say, "What the hell man?"

Instead, I saw Mab's reflection in the visor of his helmet as I hissed out in her voice, "Unhand me! How dare you lay hands on the Winter Lady!"

What the actual fairy humping fuck? I just stared at my reflection until he and a female Goblin took my arms and started leading me out of the alley to a waiting prisoner transport. Wait a minute, how did they know Mab was here? I closed my eyes in realization. Of course, the deceitful Winter Lady had likely called in an anonymous tip. And it wouldn't have been a lie to say the Queen of the Unseelie was in the alley behind Stacks since she technically had been.

I looked through the windows of the diner, seeing my reflection, looking every inch the arrogant yet unnervingly beautiful Queen of the Fae. Rory stood and watched as I was escorted into the transport, confusion and worry on her face. At least I knew she hadn't been in on her mother's plan.

When read my rights as we headed toward Beta-Stack Brigade Headquarters, I found myself answering as Mab would, complete with threats to turn them all into ice sculptures for the halls of Ha'real.

What did Mab have to gain by this? And she had to know whatever glamours and spells she had laid on me would wear off in a couple of days. Then I remembered what she said. This gained her time to figure out what was happening. Which had the unfortunate side effect of me believing that whatever Titania said about Mab being the only other person with access to Ember, may have been in error. But that's what my investigation would uncover, and I can't exactly investigate anything while I'm being detained.

I asked in frustration to the air, "Mother? A little help here?"

She responded in a tinny tone, "I'm sorry, but protocol dictates I am not to communicate with any citizen who is currently bound by law."

Well, fuck me sideways. I sighed, "Fine, then can you at least play me some music until this whole mess can be straightened out."

She didn't respond, but a tune from the archaeological archives started playing in the back of the armored vehicle.

I rolled my eyes and groaned when Stray Cat Strut by the Stray Cats started to play.

I laid my head back on the wall and muttered, "Smartass," as we navigated through the rush hour traffic of Irontown.

CHAPTER 5
She's Got the Look

In a whirlwind, I found myself in an interrogation room back at headquarters, in magic dampening cuffs, while they tried to locate 'Lieutenant Shade' to question me. Every time I tried to tell them who I was, I said 'Queen Mab'.

I was so going to fuck her up the next time I saw her, Queen of the Fae be damned!

I looked at the cuffs and almost chuckled. The more I learned about the Greater Fae the more I knew about their magic. The key thing was that, as the cuffs proved, the castings of any Fae only worked on Fae or creatures less powerful than the caster.

So while these cuffs might work on any lesser Fae or any race less powerful than the Greater Fae... any Greater Fae more powerful than the apprentice or journeyman who had spelled the cuffs wouldn't be affected. Else the spells Mab had currently cast on me would have been circumvented by the cuffs.

Commander Reise came in after a couple of hours, his stern look had an edge of nervousness to it as he stood by the door rather than joining me at the table. He was being overly cautious. I understood, if I was in a room with who I thought was the most magically powerful person on the world, one known to have a hair-trigger, and was questioning as a suspect in a crime, I'd be hesitant too.

Only I wasn't Mab.

He said as he looked at the pad he was holding as information scrolled across it, "Queen Mab, we're having a problem locating Lieutenant Shade to begin our questioning." The man looked up from the pad, eyes narrowing a bit as he asked leadingly, "I don't suppose you've seen her today?"

I sighed, meaning to say, "In the mirror this morning like every other day," but what came out was, "Oh my, you've misplaced your venerable pet human and suspect me of what? Something nefarious?"

He shook his head, "Witnesses say that they saw you in the alley behind Stacks with her this morning, but nobody saw her leave, and there was some sort of massive magical interference so none of the cameras or sensors in all of Irontown were operational during this meeting you had with her."

"What are you saying, Commander? Don't be coy, just make your accusation." Then I chuckled in that slightly unhinged way Mab had about her.

The man sputtered, sweat on his forehead as he looked back toward the door like he might bolt at any second. "I'm not accusing you or the Winter Court of anything, majesty. It is just that, Shade and Keller were tasked to bring you in for questioning because someone implicated you in the arson case in the Alpha-Stack last night. Shade's disappearance is... suspect."

"Oh my dear child, you truly are accusing me of wrongdoing, how delightful. What do I get from playing this game when you learn just how wrong you were? I don't have many Centaurs adoring my halls..."

Reise went positively pale, and he swallowed, hard, he said in a strained tone, "Nobody is accusing you of anything. We just have a few questions and I'm sure everything will be cleared up and you will be free to go."

I shook my head. "Poor child, I'm free to go at any moment." I held my hands up in the cuffs. "Do you believe for one moment that these bracelets, spelled by a bottom tier journeyman, could contain my power, or that my Fae strength couldn't snap them like toys? I wear them only for your peace of mind. And I'm sure that if I am under arrest as the Enforcers who read me my rights had indicated, that you wouldn't attempt to ask me anything without legal counsel present."

I glared at him as my mouth kept working, spitting out her words in her voice. "I'm well aware of the remedies in the legal codes that pertain to wrongful detainment of Fae Royalty. And believe me... Commander Malcolm Tiberius Reise, I will seek out and enforce each remedy to the fullest extent."

He knew he was in danger, and stayed almost impossibly still, like any movement he made would cause the apex predator in front of him to pounce and swallow him whole. "I was not aware legal counsel had not been offered to you yet. And you aren't under arrest or being accused of any crimes. We just needed to..." He blurted, "I can contact your legal counsel for you, majesty, who should I com?"

The man just lied through his teeth and I found it amusing that he even tried. The real Mab wouldn't have bought his 'oops' act. And I found that Mab's Gaes and spells hadn't thought of everything, since I just blinked at him, not having the slightest clue who Mab's lawyers were. I'm sure the Winter Court had lawyers specifically for such an instance. The only name I knew that was of any consequence wasn't a lawyer. But maybe if she met with me she'd see right through her mother's magic. "My daughter, Princess Aurora of the Unseelie."

Then I prompted as he started to turn, "And do something about these unless you want them frozen and shattered into a thousand pieces?" I held the cuffs up. I knew the Greater Fae were insanely strong, Sindri had broken bones just grabbing me, and I had no doubt that Mab could have just snapped the metal like it was made of tissue even without magic. But me? I was only human. The servos in my armor could probably break them if I strained for a while.

He inclined his head. "Of course, but I would ask you not to leave this room until you are released. Can we bring you anything to drink or eat while I contact the princess?"

I shook my head as he looked up to the ceiling, "Mother? Release."

With a click, the cuffs fell off my wrists and onto the table as Mother said in her mechanical tones, "Magic dampening cuffs released." The man was afraid to step up to me to collect them, smart if I had actually been Mab.

I sighed as I heard myself saying, "Delightful, now run along before I get bored."

The commander stepped out and I heard the same type of titanium mesh alloy locks engage that were used in blast doors. They'd hold against anyone except a Greater Fae. I witnessed Rory blow a hangar bay blast door out of its frame when she and the others came to rescue me from Lord Sindri.

I sat there, staring at the plastic ceramic window that was currently mirrored on this side, the observation room on the other side. It was so disconcerting to see Mab sitting where I was, moving when I did. My armor, which I could feel myself wearing, looked like her robes in the reflection. She truly was an impossibly beautiful woman and that was the weirdest thing about this damn spell.

As convincing as it was, it didn't carry that... power... that you could feel when looking at her. So I was amazed it was actually fooling anyone. Then again, not everyone could feel magic like me. I tried to activate my armor's systems but they remained powered down, like the magic was severing the connection between it and Mother.

Mother... "Hey, Mother?" I couldn't say what I wanted to I tested the limits of the gaes on me, the best I could say was, "Tell me a story?" Nothing, "Come on, you heard horse-butt say I wasn't under arrest. You're allowed to speak to me now, so your silent treatment is a little immature don't you think?"

There was an uncharacteristic pause like she was thinking bout what I had said. But she could make thirty-three googolplex calculations per millisecond, so it was more of her personality than actual contemplation.

I prompted, "Tell me about the first day of Exodus, the day you started the journey to Eridani Prime."

Another pause, then in her tinny tone, "I cannot find fault in your reasoning. I did record the conversation and Commander Reise had indicted you were not under arrest. What did you do with Lieutenant Shade? She is my... she is a friend of the people of the Leviathan."

I fought with the gaes and was able to at least say, "I promise that I did her no harm."

She paused one last time then started the tale of Exodus, inserting detailed time logs of initiating each system. I stopped her. "No, I don't want to hear the technical aspects of it. You are the most advanced artificial intelligence ever created, and you are capable of personal observations. We've some time to kill here, and we've never really just talked about this. I'd like to know what it was like."

She sounded confused for a moment. "You were there on the observation deck during Exodus too..." Then she caught herself and affected her artificial voice again. "It is something that goes through the unused processes in my systems frequently. I was built to be the salvation of the people of Earth. I... felt strong, big... but my morality routines keep going over the fact that as big, and strong, and voluminous as I was, we were leaving the bulk of the population of the planet behind to their own fate."

"I felt... suddenly impossibly small as I engaged the main drives to get us underway, leaving them all behind."

The last part she emoted, distracted by a memory that sounded full of shame and self-recrimination.

I offered, "What you did, what you do, is incredible. You're preserving that world that was left behind, inside of you. You should take pride in that."

Her voice was mechanical again as she said softly, "I do not wish to discuss the topic anymore. I'm running ship-wide diagnostics so I cannot spare the processing power."

Liar... this conversation was a simple memory retrieval and no computational power was used, and she could run diagnostics while juggling maintenance drones if she wanted to. The topic made her... sad.

Nodding, I consoled her, "I understand." And I did. She was full of guilt, not being... enough... to save everyone. When that was her whole purpose, why she existed, to save the people of Earth.

I understood her even more now. And it seems that her self awareness occurred long before I believed it had. She was using personal pronouns with her memories. She's been scared of revealing herself for five thousand years now? Didn't she get...

lonely?

We sat in silence for another twenty minutes before the door opened again. It was Aurora! I blurted, "Rory, thank the gods." This made her hesitate. She furrowed her brows. "Mother?"

Then she closed the door on Keller and Reise who tried to follow her into the room. With a wave of her hand, the observational window became encased in ice. "What games are you playing now? Why ask for me instead of Zinathi? You understand what you are suspected of, do you not?"

I wound up replying, "The insolent shall pay for deigning to make any accusations. Mark my words, daughter."

I moved up to her. Wanting to tell her everything but I couldn't. I reached out to grab her hands. She let go and stepped back. "What have you done with Knith? You know she is special to me, and I saw you being detained at the cafe."

In frustration, I blurted, "I'm not Mab, I'm Mab! No Mab! Fuck me sideways and space me naked."

She narrowed her eyes at me. "That's what Knith..." She took my hands again and her eyes narrowed farther. "I feel your magic, but it is a pale shadow..."

She looked to be putting things together as she asked with suspicion, "What was the first magic you taught me when I was little?"

My mouth opened but nothing came out. Again a shortcoming of Mab's magic. I couldn't answer things I didn't know the answer to. "I don't know."

"Show me your magic." Now she was smirking almost playfully.

I wiggled my fingers and said sarcastically, "Oggity boogity." Yup, that was about the extent of my magic.

She asked carefully, "Knith?" And with that, the gaes broke... so if someone figured it out on their own, then I wasn't constrained to act like Mab in front of them?

I nodded. "Oh thank the gods! Yes. I couldn't tell anyone who I was, and I kept acting like the Winter Lady. It was freaky as hells."

I went to kiss her but she put a restraining finger over my lips as she said, "Eww! You still look like my mom. Eww! Now I'm going to need an extra session in therapy." Fae went to therapy?

Mother asked, "Knith? But my sensors identify that form as Queen Mab."

I told her, glad Aurora had exposed the ruse to Mother. Now maybe I could get the hells out of here and find out what was really going on on the world.

I blurted out the whole thing, and how Mab decided to take things into her own hands to find the guilty party. We didn't need vigilantes, especially terrifyingly powerful vigilantes out there trying to do my job.

Then I said, "Ok, get me out of here, and I can get on the case."

She hesitated then said, "Not just yet. Let me see if I can't find my mother and convince her to come in first. If the Brigade goes after her, she may do something irredeemable."

"What? No, you can't..."

She leaned in to peck my lips but paused just short of me and said, "Eww." Then she stepped back out and I heard the locks cycle. "Mother fairy humper! She just left me here!"

I was disappointed and frustrated and needed to be out there, doing something, anything... I looked up to the cameras and said in resignation, "Play me something to calm my nerves, Mother?"

"I've just the thing for this occasion."

Just the thing for this... She's Got the Look by a group named Roxette started blasting in the room. I swear I heard Mother chuckling as I muttered to her, "Smartass!"

CHAPTER 6
Short Skirt Long Jacket

A couple of hours after she left, instructing the Brigade not to try questioning me until she returned, Reise came in with a plate of food fit for... well, fit for a queen. It wasn't the usual generic protein paste that was shaped like food which we normally served to detainees.

"Mind if I join you for lunch, majesty? We've been... dissuaded from any questioning until your daughter returns with, how did she put it? Enough legal weight to bring half of the Leviathan to its knees."

A smile ticked at my lips. If my... well, my girlfriend, hadn't abandoned me here, I'd have thought it humorous, and just like one would expect of a Greater Fae. She must have wondered what her mother would have said in that instance and just channeled that, because Rory... well she isn't quite like any other Fae I've met.

I was ravenous, not having had breakfast before this whole cluster fuck began. There was a pitcher of water and two plastic cups, gourmet sandwiches, fruits, and vegetables, but nothing which would take utensils to eat. Like Queen Mab would stoop to using a fork to tear out his spine. It was so absurd I almost chuckled... the Mab persona chuckled anyway. "Heavens forbid I take out your eyes with a butter knife, Commander."

He chuckled nervously and we both reached for the sandwiches, my hand landed on the one heavily laden with roast beef and cheese just before he reached it. He looked at me oddly as I took a big bite and moaned in pleasure at the mouth-watering creation. Then he reached for the one that looked to be all vegetables.

After he looked at it like it might bite him and taking an experimental nibble, he asked in a distracted tone, "I thought the Greater Fae didn't eat meat."

Mab Me's response was, "We do not. We've long since abandoned our hunting and preying on lesser animals to sustain us. Enlightenment the lesser Fae and lesser races do not share." I kept wolfing down the sandwich then froze after pouring a cup of water to wash down the huge bites.

I looked at the sandwich as I thought about what I was doing. It seemed that I was slipping up more and more as my body rejected the magics forced upon it. I grinned hugely as I attacked the sandwich. The commander was silent as he just watched me devour it until I started licking my fingers.

Sighing, Mab Me cocked our eyebrow and asked, almost in a dare, "Is there a reason you're staring at me, Commander?"

"No. No not at all, I apologize." He took another bite of the veggie sandwich and chewed mechanically as he gave a fake smile. "Mmm."

"Stop sucking up, Commander, I've seen you put away three sirloins in your office without a bit of green on your plate."

He blinked and my eyes widened a little. That was almost pure me. At this rate maybe I could shake the gaes by dinner. Now if only this stupid glamour would drop, I'd be back in business.

The man asked as he looked around, "You... you've seen me eat in my office?"

I waved off his question. He picked at the cornbread I had started to eyeball, then stood and said, "If you'll excuse me, they're pinging my coms.

The moment the door shut, Titania said to me from where she sat in the chair he had just abandoned, plucking some grapes from the platter to eat, "Mab, darling, really now. Why did you release our baby to run amuck? This is beneath you. I never thought you'd go this far." I noted that the mirrored window had become a solid wall of alloyed ceramic upon her entry.

My mouth worked as I watched her pop another grape into her mouth, catching it with her teeth then almost seductively biting it. She sighed. "I had to check on Flame to be sure you didn't do anything else rash."

I just looked at her, the Gaes wasn't helping me with anything intelligent to say. Then she seemed to deflate. "Why don't you just join me, love? It could be how it was before all the disagreements, before that... man. We were great together, and with a new world approaching, we could rule as one again." She was almost purring and I swallowed, realizing she was trying to seduce Mab. If I thought those lidded eyes and seductive smile were for me, I'd be helpless against it.

Wait. Was she implying that they had been lovers? Before whatever came between them and cause the original animosity? Which turned into a wicked and violent war after Oberon took Titania as a lover. That is what had split fairy into the Seelie and Unseelie? The Winter and Summer Courts.

The rest I knew. Oberon had offered to wed Mab to stop the war between the two courts, thinking to moderate Mab's wrath. It worked enough to stop the war, but the duplicity inherent in the Winter Court caused King Oberon to stray, to return to Titania's bed again, begetting a son... Lord Sindri. This precluded peace between the two courts forever. The Fae will never again be one people.

Oberon had had enough of both women and their inability to meet halfway, so he took the Wild Hunt on one last ride, and cast what is still considered the most powerful Gaes on the Greater Fae of both courts before he disappeared forever. It was his casting, which was rumored to have killed him, that made it so that no Greater Fae could lie. They were completely incapable of it now, causing the unfortunate result of them using the truth like a weapon to deceive in even more nefarious ways.

Mab and Titania rule as night and day, dark and light, forever equal in power. A balance that has not wavered in millennia. Though they acknowledge that the Fae need the stability of a ruler. So though each woman rules their own court, the Greater Fae as a people must have a definitive ruler. So the two queens trade off every five thousand years, being who the Fae turn to when matters affect both courts.

The most recent example was when Queen Mab, at the end of her reign, negotiated the inclusion of all the preternatural races on the Leviathan and pledged the aid of the Fae in the construction of the Worldship.

The first five thousand years of the Exodus flight, the Fae Courts were ruled by the Summer Lady. I remember when I was five and the Leviathan reached the halfway point in her journey, the handover of the mantle back to the Winter Lady. So Mab has the ultimate authority over the Fae until our arrival in the Eridani system. She'll be handing over the mantle back to Titania fifty-three years before planetfall.

I shook my head sadly at the woman, actually feeling for her. She seemed actually hurt that Mab could jeopardize the Firewyrms. She said they were their babies. Were they born of their combined magics? I said, "Don't count her out yet."

Her eyes widened after a moment, realization dawning and I hissed in pain when she was suddenly standing beside my chair, grasping my chin hard enough for me to hear bone starting to crack. She looked at me from side to side, then hissed. "You!" Then she screamed out a growling, hissing shriek, and was gone, leaving me engulfed in flame that was not flame, searing my nerves.

I sighed and realized that I was shaking as the flames extinguished. She actually scared me more than Mab did, probably because she is supposed to be the more gentle and caring of the Fae

Queens, but I haven't seen that yet. She must really hate me for what I did to her psycho son.

I pulled up a health scan to check for damage, and when a hairline fracture of my jaw was brought up I froze and realized my armor was working again. I looked to the wall that was mirrored again to see me in my armor. Titania had burned away the glamour!

The door slammed open and half a dozen heavily armed Enforcers streamed into the room with Commander Reise in the lead as he blustered at me, "Shade! What the fleeking hells? Where's Queen Mab? Where have you been?"

I held my hands up looking at the weapons swinging around in my direction. "Hey hey hey! Mab's tits guys, I'm one of you!" The commander made a hand motion and they lowered their weapons as Keller moved into the crowded room.

They all looked around like maybe Mab was hiding under a chair leg or something as I said, "Mab glamoured and gaesed me to fool everyone into thinking I was her while she went to investigate on her own. Titania was just here to talk to Mab when she realized I wasn't her, she burned off the glamour. I can still feel the gaes, but once you know who I am, I'm free to talk as me again."

Keller asked as he towered over even the commander, "The Summer Lady was here?"

I nodded. "She can apparently teleport." Then I looked at Reise. "Now can I please get the hells out of here so we can investigate this? There's a lot more to this than meets the eye."

He huffed, his nostrils flaring. "We need to debrief you as..."

I cocked an eyebrow and prompted, right on the edge of insubordination, "Mother and I will write a report up as I investigate as I was ordered to by President Yang herself." Reminding him of the meeting last night, not that I thought he would forget meeting with the President and a Fae queen.

The man nodded slowly. "When all of this is over, we're going to have a long talk in my office, Shade."

Yup, I pushed too far. Maybe I shouldn't have disobeyed in front of all these other Enforcers. I'm pretty sure I'll never learn, self-preservation seems to be an afterthought for me lately. The others seemed in shock how a mere human was talking to the commander.

I pushed past them all and told Daniel as I passed, "Can you get to Beta-B? There's something I want you to check on. I'm heading back to Alpha-B to verify the same. I'll have Mother fill you in when you get there."

He nodded and headed off the opposite direction. I had to get my Tac-Bike from Stacks. "Mother?"

She chirped in my head like she was relieved to hear from me. "I've disengaged the mag-lock and your Tac-Bike will meet us at the doors."

I prodded the bear, "Thanks, you've always got my back... except in there."

She actually pouted. "Mab cheated, my sensors were all fooled by her spells."

I snorted and cut her some slack, "It's ok, I still love you." She made a pleased sound and I prompted, "Shall we?"

"We shall." And she started playing a composition called Short Skirt Long Jacket by a group called Cake.

CHAPTER 7

Human

By the time we arrived at Alpha-B, I had already contacted Aurora, to let her know I was out. She chuckled at how put out I was about her abandoning me there. She sounded demure as she said, "I was coming back for you."

I asked, "Did you know that your mother and the Summer Lady had Firewyrms on the world?"

There was a pregnant pause before she asked, "Isn't it my turn to ask a question, Knith?"

I deadpanned. "The answer to that question is, yes. My turn."

She giggled over coms and accused, "You have to be Fae, you play this game a little too well."

"Don't deflect, did you know?"

"I am the Winter Maiden," she stated in answer.

I nodded to myself as Mother whispered in my head, "That wasn't an answer."

With a smirk I said out loud, "Actually it was an unspoken confirmation. And why are you whispering? Rory can't hear you in my head."

Ever swift on the uptake, the Fae princess teased. "Is that Mother? You don't have to pretend around me. I think it is wonderful if you are evolving, your secret is safe with me, and I cannot lie."

It was amazing how quickly Mother clammed up.

As I stepped up to the bike, I almost jumped out of my skin when Graz said from beside me, "So, where we headin', Knith? Ol' Mab really laid a whammy on you that time, didn't she?"

"Mother fairy humper! Would everyone stop sneaking up on me?" Then I looked at her as she buzzed up in front of my nose. "What are you doing here?"

She shrugged. "Mother filled me in on what was happening once the dumb tin can figured out you were you and not not you."

Mother huffed, defending weakly, "She was spelled."

Graz grinned at her needling, then said, "I figured you'd need backup."

"I don't need..."

"You got yourself landed in custody before you even started, you dumb big."

"Fair enough. But you're a civilian, and it could be dangerous, you haven't even requested a ride-along."

She shrugged and flew into my helmet before I sent the mental command for the visor to shut. "Like you said, I'm a civilian and I'm free to go wherever I want. Sue me."

I exhaled, knowing it was useless to try to argue with her, or Mother, or Rory... was there anyone on the world who listened to anything I said?

Then she asked, "So hey, does the Brigade let Sprites join? I mean, I'm doin' your job for you and not getting paid."

I snorted as I fired up the bike and shot out into traffic, and slid into the emergency vehicle lane just above the street level vessels before kicking in the afterburners with my Enforcer lights flashing. Abuse of power, I know, but I had already lost the better part of a day in my investigation, the trail was getting cold.

"You're freeloading at my place with your entire family, that's pay enough."

"You owe me."

I sputtered, "In what world do I owe you?"

"Hey, you're the one who got me evicted with all your finger-pointing and 'don't break the law' stuff. Mab's tits, woman, how's an honest Sprite supposed to survive?"

I sighed. "Would you rather I had brought you in on pilfering charges?"

I could hear her grin next to my ear where she was holding onto my hair when I did a corkscrew maneuver to dive into the spoke heading down-ring to the Trunk. The little flying pest got a kick out of getting a rise from people. Then she free-floated in front of my face to spin to look out the visor in the virtually zero-G environment of the Trunk.

"Burning fairy farts, Knith, do you have a death wish?"

What? I was only at three-quarters throttle as we ripped past the afternoon traffic. If it was rush hour, I wouldn't be opening the bike up so much.

Then as I performed another corkscrew maneuver to send us

rocketing up an Alpha-Stack spoke, I furrowed my brow and shared, "You wouldn't be able to become an enforcer. Most of the smaller races can't, and humans can barely qualify."

Before she could squeak her indignation at me, Mother shared with her, "It has to do with the physical requirements. You have to be able to lift or drag a body and move it to safety, and some residents, like the Centaurs and Minotaurs, weigh around seven hundred pounds."

I added, "Even with the help of the servos in my armor, I was barely able to qualify for that, and I'm stronger than most humans. But there are always exceptions... believe it or not, there are two leprechauns in the Brigade. One has an exo-assist skeleton like Mac has, since she comes from a D-Ring. The other, Shamus... we're still not sure how he passed. I suspect shenanigans."

I smirked and shared my suspicion, "He likely greased some palms with part of his treasure hoard. I still don't know why he wants to be an Enforcer, he's a gruff man who seems happy patrolling the trunk and D-Ring."

Graz pouted. "That's discrimination. I'm height-challenged and can't lift a stupid Big, so I can't join?"

I gave an apologetic grin. "There are other physical requirements. Not to mention I don't think they can even make scatter armor small enough to fit you, not to mention accommodating your wings."

She looked into one of my internal helmet cams, screwed up her face, and said, "She's just makin' shit up now."

Mother chuckled at her.

Graz said as we buzzed past the first two Spoke Terminals heading to our exit at the third, "But I can do things and fit in places none of the big clumsy Enforcers can."

I nodded. "Fair point." Then I smirked. "But since you can't fill out the simple form to request an official ride-along, I can't see you filling out the other forms required just to apply."

Mother and I chuckled as our Sprite friend squeaked out, "I hate you both," I tilted my head, covering her in my hair as a pseudo-hug.

Then she was screaming, "Ahhhhhhhhhh!" splatted up against my visor as I executed a final corkscrewing, maneuver to put us into the emergency vehicle lanes in the B-Ring and just kept corkscrewing.

I tried to hide my grin as I slowed to normal traffic speeds and stopped our rotation while lowering to ground level. She spun and glared at me. "A little warning?"

Placing a hand on my chest as we flew along, I mocked surprise, "Did you just call yourself little?"

"What? No! You're asking for a whupping!"

I grinned and said, "Hush, I've got work to do. Mother, can you review the last six months footage of the foot traffic here in Bulkhead J, next to the Skin. Isolate any footage with Mab. Do a similar review for Beta-Stack-B in the same region and forward it to

Lieutenant Keller? Tell him to investigate any area Mab frequents there, please?"

"On it, Knith." Then she paused. "You're looking for the Firewyrm pens. But I can tell you there are no such pens on the world. My scans are conclusive."

"Yes, but Summer and Winter are hiding them somewhere."

She seemed to contemplate it then asked, "Shall I look for Queen Titania in the same area?"

I shook my head. "No... she can teleport as she has demonstrated frequently. Depending on her range, she could be anywhere when she visits the pens."

She seemed put out I wasn't just taking her word that there were no pens, and she offered instead, "The most likely location for the Firewyrm pens are in the palaces since I'm not allowed to scan there, nor follow any of the Greater Fae inside of them."

I countered, "I doubt it because all the damage was done down here in B. I'd wager a month's food stipend that the pen is close to where we found Ember." That made me ask, "The crime scene techs and fire marshal should already have detailed reports in. Where did the fires start?"

The instant response was, "Airlock B-38 Slash A. Data shows explosive decompression in the area for seven seconds until blast doors were sealed, but the fire had spread into the corridor by then."

"Do we have video?"

"Too much magic interference. Three seconds of audio." She

played it and it sounded like a fire tornado... or like a young animal in distress...

I contemplated it. "The explosive decompression should have sucked the fire into space, but instead it moved into the corridors before the blast doors could contain it? It was Ember... any casualties reported from the decompression?"

Relief spread when she said, "There weren't many people in J when it occurred, five minor injuries and ten cases of smoke inhalation." Thank whoever is watching over us that nobody was spaced.

Thinking about the scorched hull I saw on the Skin from space, I asked. "Point of ignition? Inside or outside the airlock door?"

"Indeterminate, it was melted into slag."

Then I asked, "What Airlock had I come in when we responded to the emergency?"

"Airlock B-37 Slash A"

Counter-rotation... one section, that scorching was near the other airlock. I stopped the Tac-Bike at the scene of the fire and mag locked it as I got off and raised my visor. Engineers and construction crews were already removing the rubble and damaged portions of the decking.

How could one frightened being do all of this damage inadvertently? I understood why no fire beings were allowed passage if this was all simply a tragic accident. I could imagine if Ember had really been on a rampage. But what is done is done, she's on the world now.

The answer to my next question took me by surprise. "Can you display the hull damage by that airlock? I got a good look as we were coming in." She played back my visual records and all I saw was some blackening around the airlock near the one we docked at... there was no long scorched area.

I re-specified, "No I need the footage from when Myra flew me over to Alpha-Stack."

"This is that footage."

I pointed in the air at the display in my vision. "No, there was heavy scorching on the armor plating for at least forty feet or more."

She assured me, "I detected no evidence of this, and these are the visual records."

My suspicion was putting things together. Few things could cause such an aberration in Mother's records, magic being at the very top of that list. Something was affecting her sensors and even visual records of that area of the hull. Smirking I asked, "I assume you've isolated Mab's visits, and they were in the vicinity of Airlock B-38 Slash A?"

I did a double-take at Graz's smug look as she hovered in front of me. "What?"

"She ain't gonna find any sign of Mab. She'd never willingly go into Summer Court territory. That's just..."

Mother interrupted, "I have multiple occasions of the Winter Lady in Alpha-B Bulkhead-J corridors. It seems she goes there every Friday afternoon before sensors in the area are interrupted. An hour later, when video and sensors are restored, she leaves the area."

Graz's mouth worked like a fish out of water. I brought a finger up to gently close her mouth as it hung open.

I nodded and asked, "Same thing in Beta-Stack?"

"Yes. Always Friday, and we lose sensor records for an hour."

Graz was catching on, even though she couldn't believe Mab would go willingly into the rival court's territory. Titania had done that just to attend her son's spacing, but I cannot remember any other time that she was reported in Beta-Stack... other than her appearance in the interrogation room today.

My dust sifting sidekick said, "I suppose the Summer Lady does something similar?"

I shook my head before Mother said, "Negative."

Putting a hand palm up for her to land on as I headed to the barricades. "Titania can teleport, so she probably never shows up outside of her palace unless she wants to be seen." I wondered why Mab couldn't teleport.

I shared with the class, though I knew Mother had already figure it out too. "I'm sure that we'll find the hidden firewyrm pens by those airlocks."

I scrolled through the emergency repair logs to see that the hull breach had been sealed with a breach dome until the engineers determined what was needed to repair the airlock. So the sealed areas were open.

By the time I badged myself through the demolition zone and we picked our way back to Bulkhead J, I was putting together the next steps in the investigation since I was already positive of what we would find, or rather, not find. As much as it terrified me, I needed to get out on the Skin to examine that scorched area.

Sure enough, I studied the ship's schematics as we arrived at the damaged airlock. Even ceramic surfaces in the area were burned to dust. Ember packed a hell of a hot magical punch. About forty feet down the corridor, I found a door that wasn't on the plans. I prompted, "What's behind this door? Mother?"

In unison, Mother and Graz asked as if I had a screw loose, "What door?" It was hard for me to focus on too, so I assumed it was under one hell of a don't look here spell. And I could feel power coming off the door and knew it was heavily warded, even more so than the palace wards at the two courts.

I pushed on the wards, my scatter armor sparked brightly, and I wound up blinking and groaning in pain when I found myself almost embedded in the wall at the opposite side of the corridor. Yup, they packed a wallop all right. I said weakly, "Ow."

The workers in the area came rushing over. I held a halting hand up. "I'm ok." Then as an afterthought, I asked, "What do you see right there?"

I pointed at the door and the man and woman said, "Bulkhead?" I waved them back to work.

Standing at the door, I asked Mother to pinpoint my location. Then I walked to the other side of the door and asked how far I had moved. She replied, sounding confused at the question, "You're standing in the same spot. But I tracked your movement visually..."

That made me grin. "Ok, so this is where Ember lives. Let's see just how big this pen is. I'm going to walk side to side, let me know when my location shows I have moved."

Graz said to mother behind her hand, "I think the Human has gone space-happy."

Mother ignored her then said, "There." I nodded and walked the other way. "There."

I looked between the spots and nodded. "Ok so about twenty-five yards." Then I crossed the corridor and started walking along the wall and asked, "Now?"

She said, "I'm tracking your full movement"

I pointed at the door. "So we know they are somehow blocking you with magic or..." I furrowed my brow. "Or with code? Mother calculate the diameter of the bulkhead corridor, skin side and envelope side. Does the math add up? According to you, it should be twenty-five yards shorter than it really is."

I could almost imagine her shaking her head as she answered carefully, understanding what I was driving at. "No, it adds up properly." Then she blurted, "The bitches! They've messed with my code!"

Chuckling I said, "Welcome to my world. The Fae are always

messing with everyone. How deep is the bulkhead here?"

She growled, "Seventy-five yards."

"So behind this door is a pen a hundred and fifty feet by two hundred and twenty-five feet. It has been literally coded out of existence in your core. It has to have life support and power, can you trace that?" I asked.

She sounded smug when she said, "Yes. It was just part of the point zero zero one percent variance margins so I've never noticed it until now. Power and life support are being routed to the void in that area."

I looked at the workers and saw a Fae suit looking at plans with a job master. He must have been the Summer Fae Lord assigned to assist from the A-Ring. Or he was just a lesser Fae Lord who lives in the B-Ring here.

He saw me looking his way and I motioned him over. The man stepped up, looking impossibly beautiful like all Fae, "Yes Enforcer?" He cocked an eyebrow as he appraised me, seeing I was human with a look of distaste.

I pointed. "Can you see the don't look here right there." I pointed at the door.

He looked but I could see his eyes slide off of it to look beside the door. "There's nothing there, human."

I said, "Then you wouldn't mind touching the wall here?" I pointed and he moved aside and started to reach out. I said as I hovered my hand just shy of the wards, "No. Look at where my hand is and where you are reaching. Do they look like the same thing to you?"

He furrowed his brow, then looked at his hand as if it were the one not complying. He moved beside me and I could see a concerted effort for him to keep his eyes on my hand as he reached forward.

The man was blown across the corridor, his body actually denting an access cover, his hand was smoking, sizzling in both fire and ice. I nodded. So that was why even I couldn't step through it, both the Queens had pooled their power to create the wards.

The man groaned and I offered a hand and pulled him up as his other hand healed. I gave him a toothy grin as he tried to focus on the wall while he rubbed his hand. "Thanks for helping me test a theory, your assistance has been invaluable, citizen."

He didn't even seem to notice the insult, me calling him citizen instead of Lord. As he glared at the wall beside the door. I pointed and grinned again, hooking my thumb at the door. "Don't look here." Then I made a shooing motion to him. He walked off, vexed that he couldn't see or feel what I had.

Mother sounded amused as she whispered, "Did you just use a Fae Lord as a guinea pig?"

I snorted and said, "Investigative research, besides, I knew he'd heal up right away." I absently worked my sore jaw, knowing the hairline fracture would be healed by the morning. Part of the surprise genetic tinkering Rory had done to my embryo.

Graz wasn't repentant either as she shot me a toothy grin and two thumbs up. She wasn't a fan of the Greater Fae either since they treated her kind like vermin. "I wanted an encore. Grade A quality comedy right there."

I winked at her. We were so bad. "So we know, with that demonstration, that the wards were erected by both Mab and Titania, and not even Greater Fae can see or cross the wards. So that means what?"

Graz offered helpfully, "That Mab is guilty! I'm going to go steal something so I can go down to work in the mines just to see her doing manual labor."

I shook my head. "No, it just means that there are two persons of interest so far, as the two Ladies of the Courts appear to be the only ones that can cross the wards. I doubt I can get any of their twenty-seven children to test them like Lord Snooty there did. But we can rule out that anyone let Ember out here, so that leaves about twelve million possibilities since I know where she got out. Hells, it could have been a complete accident that Ember herself caused. I won't know until I get out there."

Mother said as if she just realized my reasoning, though I'm sure she was thirty steps ahead of me in examining the corridor. "This area of the corridor is undamaged, no scorch marks."

I winked at the camera in my helmet and touched my nose. Then Graz said as if she had figured it out too, "Ohhh, yeah. I was gonna mention that. Didn't want either of you to feel like you were dim-witted or anything."

I cocked an eyebrow and locked her lips, making a show of throwing away the key. She flipped me off, then landed on my shoulder. Then I prompted, "Mother, I'm going to need a ride."

She sighed heavily, a great trick since computers didn't breathe, "It is an unnecessary risk, Knith. Maybe you could..."

"Mother?"

"Fine. I just worry that you take too many chances." Then I could almost hear the smirk in her tone as she said, "Request sent to Commander Udriel."

I blurted, "For fuck's sake, Mother! A tug, a Brigade Crawler, or Skin Jockey rig would have been fine."

She was unrepentant, "It's what you get for taking unnecessary risks. Princess Aurora is not amused either."

"Rory?" My eyes were wide in panic.

"Yes, she requested I keep her apprised if you ever did anything to jeopardize your safety. This qualifies."

I looked between the camera and Graz on my shoulder, looking for support. The Sprite shrugged. "Hey, don't look at me. I'm with them. You get yourself splatted in space, I lose my home."

I muttered to space, "Are all the women in my life bound to betray me?"

"Yup."

"Pretty much."

Benedict Sprite pointed out helpfully. "You whine a lot, even for a human, Knith." Mother made a sound of agreement and I just sighed. I'd never win.

Mother provided, "Commander Udriel's ETA at Airlock B-38 Slash A is four minutes fifty-three seconds." I sighed then turned and started double-timing it down the corridor as I grumbled under my breath.

I sighed as I started to contemplate all the ways past the wards. It would depend on how far they extended. Just across the door or around the entire pen. I could think of two offhand, and possibly three depending on what we find outside of the world.

My instincts were already telling me the how, it was just the who that I needed to work on. Just from what little I have seen, it looks as though Ember was somehow on the outside of the ship and melted her way into the airlock. It made sense with the impressions I got from her about the 'big black', that had to be space.

The list of millions just got knocked down to a few groups. But who would have a motive? What would they gain in releasing a baby Firewyrm? And what made me sick to my stomach was that maybe releasing her into the ring wasn't the plan at all, what if they had meant to space Ember instead, but she was able to hang onto the hull without being flung off by centrifugal force into the unforgiving vacuum.

That thought enraged me. I know I had only just met her, but my impression of her is that she was very sweet and childlike. I don't care if she is over five thousand years old, who would do that to a child?

I went through the list of people with access to EVA suits or remote maintenance drones. Brigade Enforcers, Engineering Corps, Skin Jockeys, and the Ready Squadron. That was still thousands of possible suspects. Plus the unlikely possibility Ember had somehow burned through her pen herself and found herself in the big dark as she puts it. Somehow I doubt the Summer and Winter Ladies would be so careless as to leave an area in her pen where Ember's magic could burn through the hull.

My coms were pinging and I sighed, squinted an eye and answered, "Hi Rory."

"Don't hi Rory me. Mother told me what you're about to do. You can dispatch a Brigade Crawler to investigate with EVA qualified techs."

It was true, I could, but I hadn't ruled anyone out fully, not even the Queens, no matter how unlikely all these choices were. "I'm a hands-on investigator. And we're only going out for a look. I promise I won't leave Commander Udriel's ship."

After a pause, her voice sounded odd. " Commander Udriel? As in your ex?" Was she jealous of someone I dated literally half my lifetime ago?

I couldn't help but grin. "Why Aurora Ashryver, are you jealous?" She looked at her camera then cut to audio-only, but I had already seen the blush.

"I'm not jealous. You just take too many chances." She paused.

"And there are hundreds of other pilots you could have called."

Tongue in cheek I shared, "It was Mother who called her, it wasn't my idea. It's sort of awkward for me."

She didn't say anything about that, instead, she changed the subject. "I see you got yourself out of custody. Commendable."

"Umm... actually it was, umm, the Summer Lady. She thought I was Mab for a moment, she wasn't happy when she figured out it was me. And for some reason, she's mad at me about it like it was my idea or something."

She asked, "Why would she come to see my..." She trailed off to silence, speaking volumes.

I prompted as I arrived at the airlock, "How much do you know about the Firewyrms? I've got a hypothesis as to why both of the Queens are so concerned about them."

Again, her silence told me she either suspected or knew. I nodded to myself and told her, "If you can locate her before me or Mother in her scans, tell her to leave the investigation to me or she'll make a bigger mess of things. I have a hunch I'm close to figuring out who did this, I just need to gather the facts to shake the tree a bit."

She reactivated video and said, "Fine. I've learned your hunches border on the improbable, I'd like to think I had something to do with that."

Chuckling I told her, "You sound just like a Fae,"

"Mother, what is the proper response in this situation?"

The traitorous AI replied, "Smartass would be the proper vernacular."

Graz unlocked her lips and offered, "If we stick with posterior descriptions, then asswipe works too. And we all know Knith has a weird thing about asses." Her eyes bulged in alarm at the death glare I shot her and she mimed zipping her lips, then locking them then... was that plasma bonding?

Ignored all of their needling, I said, "Gotta jet, Myra is docking now."

Before I could close the channel, Rory said in a quieter tone, "Be careful."

Sighing I nodded slowly. "See you soon." Then I closed the channel. "Whose side are you on Mother?" I grumped.

"Normally yours, but I agree with her, you take too many risks."

Graz nodded, grinning and making a show of keeping her lips together. I looked at her. "Oh you'd take Rory's side even if she was wrong, you've got Princess worship." She nodded eagerly. Great, so much for loyalty.

I straightened up when the airlock doors cycled, revealing a catlike human, tail twitching in amusement. "Twice in twenty-four hours, Shade? I'm not a taxi service you know, I've a job... an important one."

I sighed and hung my head, shaking it as I defended again, "It wasn't my idea to call you, Mother took it upon herself." Then I narrowed my eyes. "What kind of shifts do you rocket riders work anyway? It was late last night you ferried me before."

She sighed, though her lips did quirk in a grin at the slang people used for the Ready Squadron pilots. She thumbed her chest and almost yowled out, "Ready Squadron, remember? Twenty four hours on, twenty-four hours off since we are perpetually short-handed. We shoot the shit before it hits the fan?"

I chuckled at the old slogan since they literally had to shoot any incoming celestial debris big enough to damage the Skin. If they missed, we'd be hip deep in the shit as the ship's systems contained any hull breaches.

Bowing I offered, "After you, kitty cat."

She lifted her nose regally and marched back into the airlock with us following. "That armor doesn't look anything like the Enforcer gear I'm used to seeing."

"Experimental nano-panels."

"Ah, like ours. How quaint, the Brigade is always five years behind." The inner airlock door cycled closed.

"At least we're not space-mad rocket jocks." Ahh, the friendly rivalry between the Brigade and the Squadron.

Her tail whipped behind her and she yanked my feet out from under me as she hit the controls to cycle the outer doors. "It looks good on you." She looked over her shoulder and cocked her eyebrows when I regained my footing before I landed on my ass.

She shook her head. "You've still got those reflexes, you've got to tell me someday how you do that."

I flipped her off, she chuckled as we stepped into the ship and sealed the ship and strapped into the cockpit seats. "I'm not fast, you're just..."

"...slow? Fine, keep your secrets. My reflexes are enhanced by my implants and I'm still not sure I could recover that fast. Hang on."

We left my stomach somewhere behind us as we almost exploded away from the Skin. She asked, "Destination?" as she started to align us for another parabolic flight path.

I winged my thumb. "Next airlock over please."

She chuckled and stared at me expectantly. "Wait, you're serious?"

I nodded. "I need to check out the scorch on the Skin near it. We need to get close."

"You mean the micrometeorite strike? It's... oh, you think it had something to do with the fire?"

Nodding she said, "Ok, let's get inverted." The vessel snapped over one-eighty like it were on a spindle, and instead of flying above the Ring, my perspective changed as my mind now interpreted what I was seeing as flying below the ring.

I muttered, "Everything is just a matter of perspective," as I looked up out of the clear canopy at the ring. It looked so massive this close to it. Like it went on forever, curving over its own horizon. I looked down from the side window to see the A-Ring now below us at this perspective, looking even more massive. Well duh, it is more massive Shade.

As we passed over the emergency breach dome that was fastened to the skin over the damaged airlock, she said, "Hmm... where is it? I swear it was right here. Did the skin jockeys already get it cleaned up?"

"Can you get us closer?" I asked.

She nodded and with uncanny precision, after shutting off the proximity alert alarms, she brought the canopy within a couple of feet of the Skin.

I swallowed and said, "Good. Can you head a few yards sympathetic rotation?" We looked as pristine diamond-hard alloy, mesh, and photovoltaic scales rotated past, mating up with some that were slightly less than pristine.

Rationalizing to myself, I muttered, "Some of the panels have been replaced. The skin jockeys have cleaned up the area."

She nodded and I asked myself, "What are the odds?"

Mother said, "There were no scheduled repairs in this area. Statistical probability of it being as serious as the blown airlock are seventeen thousand, three hundred and three, to one."

"It was rhetorical, Mother." Then to Myra, I asked, "Redheads, am I right?"

Mother harrumphed. I have always pictured her as a testy but helpful redhead in a professional suit and glasses, sitting behind a desk and pulling strings for my cases, a smirk on her face.

Myra's catlike features scrunched up in confusion. "Redheads?

She's an AI. Did she just harrumph?"

"No."

"You're right, I'm going space-mad."

I chuckled and told her. "Thanks for the ride, I have what I needed, I know what my next move is now. If you could just drop me where you found me."

"In that Irontown Grunge bar, where you were singing off-key karaoke with what was she, a wolf shifter?"

"She was a Faun, thank you very much. She wound up going home with some pretty half-elf who promised to show her the size of his tree. And no, smartass, the airlock. You know what I meant."

She half chuckled half purred in amusement.

A minute later we docked again. I stepped into the airlock and turned to thank her again just to have the airlock door cycle in my face. She grinned as she flipped me off through the window. Ok, she was still as funny as she thought she was.

I found myself comparing her to Aurora and found there was no comparison. I was one lucky human. Then I got back on task. "Mother?"

"Checking all flight logs of all External Maintenance Crew ships and repair logs."

"Great, can you..."

"Already informed the External Maintenance Crew shift commander for this sector to expect you within the hour."

"What would I do without you?"

"Likely die screaming in space."

I chuckled and agreed, "Likely." Then the smartass started playing Human, by the Human League in my helmet.

CHAPTER 8

I Wanna Be A Cowboy

We made our way back out to the Tac-Bike, pausing in Bulkhead H by some repair crews where a woman sat in the shadows, avoiding the light filtering in from the Day Lights outside in the massive hole Ember had burrowed through the ten bulkheads.

A vampire? Here? They rarely venture above the D or C rings and prefer the shadowed corridors close to the Skin as UV light gives them a nasty sunburn and hurts their eyes. Even star shine from the nearby nebula hurt their eyes at night.

"Ma'am, are you alright? What are you doing here in the corridor?" I asked.

She leaned forward, shielding her eyes with her arm. I often forget how attractive healthy vampires are. Like Gemma, the only Vampire in the Brigade, who taught Defense Against Vampires at the academy. They were hunters before the Exodus and used a glamour that is minor compared to the Fae to put the mental whammy on their prey before they feed. But now, on the ship, they got daily blood rations from Med-Tech.

She backed up a bit, the reaction most vamps had when an Enforcer was around. She pulled out her ration card, holding it up to me. I didn't bother scanning it to ensure she was using the blood provided her and not supplementing it with some illegal night hunting. Her clothing was high end if wrinkled a bit and she had an air of sophistication about her.

I waved her off. "Ma'am?" I still didn't know why any human would choose to become a vampire, it seemed shallow to trade your humanity and life under the lights of the Rings just for eternal youth. Especially with the risk of going feral. But I guess it was like witches and power, as Humans were never meant to have magic, and there was a price. There's a reason most of the stories you hear about witches describe them as old, wrinkled, crones. That power slowly drains their own life-force.

Vamps and Witches were an almost infinitesimal branch of humans when compared to the shapeshifter population, which was still less than one percent of the Human population on the world. Most of the other races didn't bother differentiating between branches.

The woman focused on me and pocketed her blood ration card and stood in that overly graceful manner her kind was known for. She motioned to the group of destroyed quarters. "That was my home... It's gone. The engineers think it will be weeks if not months before they get to rebuilding it. I don't have family on the World and don't know where to go. The shelters in the Alpha-Stack are all full of displaced people and families from the fire."

I sometimes lose track of the impact which tragedies like this have on the citizens. It is a real toll that affects real lives or un-life in this case. Whoever caused all of this probably isn't even thinking of the people who lost their homes and everything.

I furrowed my brow. "I'm sorry, but I have to ask, you live on the B-Ring? The Fae are kind of particular who they allow in the A-Rings and have a lot of influence on who their neighbors are in the B-Rings. And even though you're a vampire, that still equates to human for them."

She actually chuckled and nodded. "Very true. But I'm a botanist, I tend their night-blooming flowers by the lake just a quarter-mile from the fire. I have value to them because there are breeds of flowers who shy away from people without magic in them. The flowers don't react to me as I'm not exactly alive."

Ok, her toothy and sheepish grin, showed a little fang. And the part of my brain that recognizes a predator was pinging. I pushed it down. All Vampires were predators, but so was I, so I grinned back at her self deprecation.

I supplied, offering my hand, retracting my gauntlet. "Knith. Lieutenant Knith Shade."

She looked at me, cocked an eyebrow and then shook my hand with her delicate looking room temperature hand, being careful not to crush my bones. "You're not afraid?"

"Should I be?"

"No. It's just refreshing. Not many humans dare to speak with us, let alone let us touch them. Unless they're playing out some blood fantasy on the Remnants of course." She shuddered in distaste at that, though her eyes did get decidedly darker at the mention of fresh blood.

"I'm not many humans."

"I can see that." Then she offered, "Victoria Morgan"

I nodded then nudged my chin toward her wrist console, she held it up to me and I typed into the virtual console as I said "This is the contact information for Thase Tanda. A Vampire in Beta-Stack C. He owes me a favor and has a new place. He's a recovering feral but has been off live blood for a few weeks now. He can put you up until your place is re-built."

She blinked, her eyes going black as she cocked her head. "That's surprisingly thoughtful of you."

I shrugged. "To protect and serve, ma'am." I tipped an imaginary hat and she chuckled at me then stepped back into shadow as she said, "Maybe I'll look this Tanda up when night falls."

I nodded and asked, "Do you need blood until then? I can have a Med-Tech courier deliver some on your card." A hungry vampire isn't always a safe vampire.

"No, I fed just before the fire last night. But thank you, Lieutenant Shade."

I nodded and then continued out to the bike. We were three bulkheads away by the time Graz came out of hiding. "You're certifiable, Knith."

Nodding I verified, "Probably, but she's a citizen too. We can't just pick and choose which people in need that we help. And where were you, micro scaredy-cat?"

She buzzed up to hover in front of my face. "I was nestled down in the promised land. I wasn't scared, I coulda taken her."

I cocked an eyebrow at the promised land quip, but I didn't doubt her assertion that she could take a vamp. I had seen it with my own eyes once. I had no clue that Sprites could vary the spectrum and intensity of their light except to hide it. She had burned Thase into submission by flaring up in the ultra-violet spectrum.

Then Mother snorted when Graz crossed her arms over her chest, narrowing an eye dangerously. "And did you just call me small?"

I shook my head as we arrived at the bike, and she zipped into my helmet as my visor snapped up. "Of course not, your head is bigger than all of ours combined."

"Stupid null."

"Flying rat."

"Children!"

Graz and I said sheepishly, "Sorry, Mother." Wait, did the Leviathan just chastise me? Grr, why was I grinning?

"Oh, could you please..." I asked.

"I've already messaged Thase Tanda, reminding him that he owes you, and informed him that Miss Morgan may contact him."

"One of these days you're going to guess wrong when you anticipate me, woman."

Mother countered in a chirpy tone, "But today is not that day."

"No, it is not." Then I slammed the throttle wide open and we shot toward the Spoke, Graz screaming all the way.

I wondered if the commander of the skin jockeys in the Alpha-Stack was as much a piece of work as Commander Lincoln in Beta. That woman was an old bitter human who was over fifty percent modded. Just one or two replacement parts away from going full cyber like Mir.

Being a skin jockey was hard and thankless work. Cleaning the hull and repairing strike damage or structural weaknesses, spending hours at a time in EVA suits, tugs, and exoskeleton walker rigs out in the vacuum of space. And their careers were usually short, with a high percentage going space-mad, or becoming violent and erratic.

Commander Lincoln was a lifer, so held a lot of clout with the other skin jockeys of the External Maintenance Crews. She earned her place and everyone just put up with her eccentric temper.

"Who's the commander here in Alpha?"

Before Mother answered, Graz said as she tugged my earlobe, "Commander Hardy, a bigger pain in the ass than Mac. He makes sure every trade is to his benefit. Old fart, ornery as hell, like Mac."

Mother corrected. "He's only thirty-five, youngest of the four External Maintenance commanders."

Our Sprite companion waved that off. "Yeah yeah, I can never tell with you bigs, especially you humans who live lives shorter than a fart in space. You all look the same to me."

I corkscrewed, throwing Graz flat against the visor. She mumbled from the side of her mouth where her face was plastered to the visor, "Fair argument. Touchy touchy." I smirked and leveled out as we headed down-ring to D.

"Ornery as hell though? Mother, I'm going to need a warrant for their records if he's going to be difficult."

She replied absently, "I know a friendly judge who owes me. You'll have them before we reach our destination."

How does a judge owe her? How does she have her virtual fingers in so many pies? There were so many questions I wanted to ask her, and now I had about a dozen more.

Before long we arrived at what looked like a scrapyard in front of a section of Bulkhead A in the lower gravity D-ring. I knew that Graz and other scavengers would pick through this mess like the ones in the other stacks, eeking out a living selling any viable parts they could salvage from the discards.

I knew behind the huge bay doors on the bulkhead, was a storage and hangar bay that extended all the way to the back of the ten bulkheads to the skin, where dual hangar doors which were like a huge airlock allowed the maintenance tugs out with the pristine replacement parts stored in the massive, cavernous space.

Skin jockeys were paid by the day, as they had almost a revolving door of turnaround. A lot of down on their luck citizens would take the job for a day or two, sometimes making it a full week under the command of the veterans. I saw the lines at the gates every morning in our stack hoping to make quick chit.

The salaried maintenance veterans were usually hardcore and were as likely to scare off the daily workers as the work itself. They often moonlighted as thugs for hire just to keep their adrenaline pumping. I had a run in with a group when I was investigating Lord Sindri. I guess back on old Earth they would be called mercenaries.

I mag-locked the bike by the smaller entry doors, and said to Graz, "If this guy knows you, you might want to keep out of sight. I don't suppose I can get you to stay with the bike?" Her snort was answer enough so I checked my gear, saw the warrant information scrolling in my peripheral vision as promised, and headed inside.

I blinked. The office area was immaculate, not covered with parts and info pads, and food wrappers like our stack's External Maintenance Crew main office. And soothing music was playing. I asked, "What is this music, Mother?"

"Jazz, from the mid-nineteen hundreds."

I liked it.

A man with an external exoskeleton strapped onto him was asleep in his chair, feet up on the desk. He snorted an aborted snore and then opened his eyes and saw me and quickly stood. He was a young man with roguish stubble on his rock hard looking jaw. His smile was warm and inviting as he said, "Enforcer Shade I presume? The Leviathan AI set up this meeting."

He gave me the grin of a scoundrel as he looked me up and down. "You're the one from all the news waves a few weeks back. Took down a Greater Fae hand to hand? Your reputation precedes you."

I liked the man, he didn't seem to take life too seriously. "Yes.

I'm here to meet with Commander Hardy, Brigade business." I tapped my badge unnecessarily.

He held his hands out to his side, beaming a winning smile. "You've found him."

Blinking, I said down into my helmet, "Really? This is the ornery old fart?"

Graz's voice squeaked out, "Always taking a cut of my profits."

The man looked at me, cocked an eyebrow. "Is that you in there Graz? You're lucky I let you off the grounds at all, you dust sifting thief. Scavenging the scrap heaps is illegal, and don't pretend you aren't sneaking off with twice as much as you say you're taking. It's all property of the world."

It was my turn to cock an eyebrow. "Extorting chits from citizens who are illegally scrapping?"

Graz buzzed out of hiding to my shoulder as the two of them blurted out in unison, "Allegedly."

"Space me now. May the gods grant me patience for lovers and fools."

The man shrugged and offered, "As of last week, I've got a new mouth to feed."

I brightened. "You've a child?" The last seven days of Human birth records for the Stacks streamed in my peripheral heads up display, three for the Alpha-Stack, and one from the Reproduction Clinic to keep Equilibrium. "Hmm... none registered to you."

The man smirked and pointed at a fluffy little bed at the foot of his chair and a ball of fur coiled up in it. "I got a guard dog to keep the riff-raff and undesirables out of the yard."

Ok, I can't be an Enforcer all the time. I melted and crouched to pet the tiny canine. It stretched and looked up at me. Its cute puppy eyes wide and its little tail thumping. "It's so cute, what is it?"

The man said with pride, "It's called a Chihuahua, I had it grown at the gene bank. Doesn't eat much and is said to be a great mouser." Mice and rats were a problem down in the D-Rings, how they got loose on a ship built in space, nobody knows. Theory has it they had stowed away on the construction and supply ships or Exodus population transports.

The rodents are a problem with the wire and cable insulation, as they find it tasty. Every effort to contain or exterminate them fails. This is why the lower rings have large cat populations as it seems to be the best way to keep the numbers down on the vermin.

I patted the Chihuahua dog, who had a little bone-shaped brass tag on his collar that read, "Spike," and its tail sped up.

Each household was allowed one pet if they desired, but no additional food rations. So usually only those who could afford supplemental foods had them, or families would have a smaller pet like this or a cat so that it didn't put too big a dent on their ration cards.

Graz zipped down to the little dog. "This is a dog? It looks like a rat with big ears. Kind of cute though, in an... eep!" The tiny thing lunged at her, sharp little teeth snapping. But Sprite's reflexes are lightning-fast and Graz zipped out of the way, drawing her pointy little blade. "Oh yeah? You want a piece of me? I'll teach you to..."

Dust sifted from her wings when I reached over and twapped her on the top of the head. "Behave, you're in his house." She growled back at the growling pup and put her blade away.

The Commander was all grins. "Ahh... money well spent. He'll do great keeping the vermin away." He looked away from the indignant lesser Fae to me. "And to what do I owe the pleasure of your company today, Enforcer Shade?"

"Knith, please. I was needing access to the flight logs and Skin maintenance records for the past twenty-four hours." I offered my wrist console to him, "I have warr..."

Before I could finish he said, "Of course..." He placed his thumb on the screen to give his authorization.

I finished, "ants..."

He beamed a winning smile. "Anything to help the Brigade. What does this pertain to?"

Ok, this was new, someone being cooperative and not caring about warrants. I usually had to fight tooth and nail just to get someone's com records. Hmm... "And com records for the vehicles assigned to your depot?"

"Of course."

I nodded in appreciation, and his verbal assent allowed Mother to access and start streaming the records as she started going through them and the flight and repair logs. "We're just investigating the fire up-ring in B, just getting our proverbial ducks in a row."

He nodded and said, "Terrible thing that. But I thought FABLE detained the Winter Lady for that."

I shrugged noncommittally. "Like I said, just getting our ducks in a row."

He looked from me to a set of doors that led to the back, then nudged his chin toward them. "Don't suppose you'd like a tour of the facility? We don't get many visitors who aren't looking for a day job or thieving from the scrapyard. Especially famous visitors. We run a tight ship down here."

Graz didn't pay attention to the insult, she was busy teasing poor Spike by buzzing past him, daring him to bite her. I told him, "I'd like that, Commander."

He waved his hand. "Max, please, were both public servants here. I'm sure you'll find some of the streamlining we do here in Alpha is groundbreaking stuff."

Ok, now he was being facetious. I rolled my eyes at his toothy grin. I liked the man. He wasn't at all like most of the skin jockeys I've met. Leaving Graz behind, we stepped through the doors and instead of the chaos of the Beta-Stack's External Maintenance Crew bay, this one was almost sedate. People moving around in an organized fashion, with drones assisting in the loading and unloading of the tugs and rigs.

Vehicles flying in and out of the giant bay doors at the end in an almost constant cycle. I always forget just how huge the scale panels they dealt with were, at least ten yards tall in a honeycomb shape, towering above us as we walked down the rows.

He pointed out some of the innovations he has implemented to make things smoother and the procedures that had been put in place to streamline any repair call. And even steps they were taking to minimize the dangers to the crews when they went EVA, like keeping the tugs between the exposed workers and the bow-shock of the Worldship, or between them and the nebula, using the vehicle radiation shields as a buffer for the workers.

Call me a geek, but I found some of it fascinating. I admit I never thought of any of it or how it impacted the mental stability or morale of the workers. The skin jockeys just... were. Like the Brigade just was. A fact of life on the world.

He introduced me to some of the veteran crews, but they were prepping for repairs so I didn't get to talk much with them. They seemed more well adjusted than most, though I could see that glint of instability in the eyes of some of the lifers that I associated with those who spent too much time outside the world. Odd the Ready Squadron rarely had cases of space madness. But I'm sure their psychological screening was much more stringent. And they got three months of paid leave per ship-year to decompress.

The hairs on the back of my neck were standing on end just as we were finishing up the tour, I glanced at one of the tugs, and the crew was watching me intently. They looked very familiar, but I couldn't place them.

My attention was drawn away from them when Spike came trotting out into the bay, whimpering. I had to blink as my brain processed what I was seeing. Graz was riding the little dog, grasping its ears in her hands, and seemed to be steering the mortified little thing.

"Graz! Get off of the poor thing!" I blurted.

She buzzed up to me and hid behind me as she said down to it, "Not so tough now, are you?" Then as she looked up to Max. "Nice try, but next time get a bigger beast."

The man scooped up his mortified pup and pointed at the door, telling Graz, "Out, flying rat."

It was so very hard not to laugh when Graz flew into my helmet and tugged on my hair as she whispered in my ear, "Can we get one of those? It's like having my own Tac-Bike." Space me now.

I muttered as we marched back into the office, "I swear I don't know why I put up with your tiny ass." Then to Max, I said, "I apologize for the buzzing jerk. And thank you for your help today... and the tour, it was surprisingly enlightening."

He cocked a finger and fired as he winked. "Not a problem. It's a refreshing change of pace."

We got out to the bike as I chastised Graz, "Would it hurt you just to be civil for like two minutes?"

She thought on it, held a finger up and said, "Yes."

Mother fairy humper. Whatever. Time to get back to work,

"Mother?"

She seemed disappointed as she said, "There are no records of any crews sent out to the vicinity of the repair. And no coms traffic in that area except the engineering corps when they placed and sealed the airlock repair dome."

I saw a glaring problem with that, and on a hunch, I asked, "Is there any record of a dispute between the Fae Courts and any of the skin jockeys? And while you're looking, can you give me a list of all the crews assigned to this depot? The skin jockeys have to be involved if there is no record since somebody had to repair the scorched skin."

"On it."

Graz teased, "She doesn't ask for much does she?"

"Shut up. You terrorized that poor pup."

She flexed a muscle in my peripheral vision and blew some glittering dust off of it while grinning at me, the unrepentant mini-jerk. Ok, so she's funny sometimes.

As we flew toward home, the Tac-Bike on autopilot, I reviewed Daniel's reports on the investigation on his side, and he had even less than us.

"Mother, play some of that antique music crap Knith likes. It gets boring when she starts digging into data and reports." Graz asked.

I snorted when a silly tune called I Wanna Be A Cowboy by a group called Boys Don't Cry started to play.

CHAPTER 9
Smooth Operator

Rory was waiting at my quarters when we arrived home. My day was looking up. Her arms were crossed and her foot was actually tapping as she stood in my main room, Graz's children swarming her hair, braiding it and putting flowers in it.

I opened my mouth but she asked, a little tersely, "What? No Commander Udriel?"

Ok, I tried not to smile at that, but failed and prompted, "Jealous?" Then I added, "How did you get into my quarters again?"

The little ones buzzed up to me and answered in unison, "We let her in!" Then they tittered over her as they went back to work.

She almost pouted, "No I'm not jealous. It just seems you're spending an awful lot of time with your ex."

"I didn't call her. And besides, I'm courting someone." I replied.

My cheeks quirked when she looked to almost ask who, when she realized I was talking about her. She lifted her nose regally. "And don't you forget it."

I set my helmet down and leaned forward to rest my forehead on hers. "Wouldn't ever want to." Then I kissed her on the nose before I trudged past. "Let me get out of my armor and we can talk."

She looked pleased with herself as I went into my bedchamber while Graz zipped around to corral her kids and usher them into the nightstand. I stepped behind my changing screen and pulled off the armor and pulled on a civilian shirt. I needed to buy more. I've been leaving my quarters more frequently since I met Rory, and I think I liked it. Though I have been spending less time training and sparring.

I walked back into the main room, and Aurora was setting some teacups on the fold-down table in front of the used sofa. She smiled and motioned for me to sit. I glanced at the kitchen area and didn't see the teapot. How had she... just don't ask, Knith. A beautiful woman just made you tea, shut up and sit down.

I sat next to her and she furrowed her brow and looked around the space. "You know, you've had these new quarters for weeks now, you can personalize it you know. Even just some real furniture would make it feel more like a home than a barracks."

Looking around I shrugged. It was pretty spartan, with the sofa I bought so that she would have someplace to sit other than the two fold-out chairs I owned. I guess it did look a little spartan. But after college, I moved into the academy dorms, then the Brigade barracks. They were all pre-furnished with the bare minimum to make them livable spaces. This was the first place I had ever lived that was a civilian space, even though the FABLE office footed the bill.

I pointed out to her helpfully. "I have my changing screen in my bedchamber." It was really the only thing I owned that could be remotely considered furniture-ish.

She furrowed her brow then moved her new silverish braided

hair to her other shoulder. "I've meant to ask you about that. It seems out of place for an enforcer, and it is heirloom quality."

She sipped at her tea, the steam tracing the delicate lines of her face and curling around her perfectly sculpted brows. I shrugged and said, "I saw some pictures from old Earth, a family preparing for a picnic, and the mother putting on a robe behind one. It fascinated me, so when I moved from student housing at the Brigade Academy and into my private quarters in the barracks, I found a woodworker in Beta-B, the first time I had ever been to a B-Ring."

"I had seen countless holos and waves of the upper rings and thought I had been prepared for the forests and all the nature that flowed in seamlessly into the towns and fields of various crops. It was almost magical to me, yet I knew what I was seeing was nothing compared with the paradises the A-Rings were."

Sipping the tea and raising a brow at it, it was a rich and soothing blend that I wasn't familiar with, I wondered where she had gotten it since it wasn't anything I had in my kitchen. I took a second sip then continued, "I located the woodworker, an Elf named J'wald, and showed him what I was looking for. He explained it was called a changing screen or vanity screen from old Earth. He had a couple in his workshop to show me. The workmanship of the hand-carved wood was exquisite and they had what he said was rice paper panels."

Lost in the memory I cocked my head and looked off into the past. "I remember almost choking when J'wald shared the price. He quickly assured me that he could recommend a shop or two down-ring that could fabricate one out of aluminum or plastic for me. He wasn't mean about it, like some of the up-ringers are to people like me, he was trying to be genuinely helpful."

She smiled and placed a hand on mine, the heat and strength of it filling me with a calm I rarely had inside. "I asked about one less ornate, that I preferred something crafted by hand, than some cold computer cut and constructed thing. And wood... wood is so rare down-ring, it has a warmth that man-made materials don't possess."

I shrugged as she laid her head on my shoulder. "So he asked what my budget was, I told him the extent of my bank balance, five years of savings and it still amounted to not even half the price of one of his screens. I remember what the Elf told me as he studied me. He had said that humans were always in such a hurry, probably because of our short lives, and rarely took the time to appreciate something an artisan pours their soul into. That it was refreshing to hear me wanting that over what was readily within my means elsewhere."

I noticed that Graz and her family had come out at some point and were all lining the fold-out table as I went on. "J'wald, looked at the picture again and told me to come back in a week, then shooed me out of his shop. I didn't know what he was doing since I knew I couldn't afford his work."

She sat up to sip her tea before snuggling back into me, her lavender eyes peering up at me. I stroked her hair which felt like spun silk in my fingers as I smiled and shared, "I returned to his shop a week later. Then a man went into the back and brought out a screen that took my breath away. The others he had paled in comparison."

I looked around at my audience who seemed enthralled by such a simple tale. "He told me to make sure to recommend his services to anyone in need of custom woodworking and asked if I needed help getting it down-ring, that he could have it shipped by courier. I had sputtered out something lame like I couldn't afford it, especially one so exquisite. And do you know what he told me? I carry it with me even today."

The Sprites all leaned in, little Twinkle zipped over to sit on Rory's hand to look up at me with wide eyes. "What did he say?"

The memory was one I held almost as a mantra inside me. "He said that it was the wish of any artisan for their work to be owned by someone who truly appreciates it, not for its value, but for the joy it gives them seeing the art for what it truly is, an extension of the artist's soul."

"Then he said simply, that money didn't matter. And that I could reimburse him by being the best version of myself in my short-lived existence before my flame burned out. And to 'Do for others what they cannot do for themselves, show kindness to those who may not be afforded it else wise. Lend aid when others cannot, and consider me paid in full.'"

Again I found myself shrugging. "So that's what I do. And that changing screen is my prized possession, if you look at the vines carved on it, they form my name in old elvish runes." I waved a hand around. "I'm not used to having so much space, and the Brigade provided everything I needed, including furniture. It is just disconcerting knowing this space is mine to do with what I want. I just don't know who I am yet to be able to fill it."

We all sat in silence for a minute, until Graz and her family quietly buzzed up into the cupboards in the kitchen to eat, giving Rory and me a bit of privacy. She nodded at me then sat up. "When all this nasty business about the fire is over, let's go out looking for furniture that fits you. We can make your quarters a home."

I nodded. "I'd like that. I guess I just hadn't noticed how empty, cold and impersonal the place was." I looked away from her, my eyes widening in sudden alarm. "Hey you dust sifting gatecrashers, keep out of the sugared cereal, the last time you were bouncing off the walls all night and I didn't get a minute of sleep." Nobody answered. I groaned.

Rory chuckled. "Come on, Knith, they're adorable, and you're sweet to take them in."

I mock grumped, "Like I had any choice." Truth be told, I actually liked having Graz's family there. It made the place feel, I don't know, not so empty maybe?

Then I smirked and shared the story of Graz conquering a poor pup and riding it like a horse. It had her tittering, eyes watering, and I felt I had accomplished something great by making her laugh. I took the opportunity to kiss her and she moaned into it, returning it with heat.

Then like an idiot, I ruined the moment after we broke it off for some air. "Were you able to find your mother?"

Like a switch was flipped, all the heat in her eyes frosted over. "Did I find her?" Space me naked. I mentally pounded my head on the table and awarded myself the bonehead trophy.

I may be dense in some ways, but I caught her answering the question with another question since she would have only been able to tell the truth. That told me what I needed to know without implicating her in harboring a fugitive. I said, "Good. I'm making progress. I'm just one motive and a little physical evidence away from figuring this whole mess out. Then she can go home."

Trying to make up for bringing work into an intimate moment, I offered, "Dinner? I can whip something up."

This put a playful smirk on her lips, "I'll pass. I know what you have in your cupboards We'll have to add grocery shopping to our list of things to do about your place."

Then she got serious and asked, "What's going to happen to Ember and Flame when all of this is over? Are they going to... to..."

I placed a hand on her arm. "I haven't included any mention of Firewyrms in my case notes, neither has Daniel. It was sort of implied by the Summer Lady that we should keep it quiet. Since only she, Graz, and me had actually seen Ember. And the President... well for as badass as I used to think she was, she'd sell her own children to the Queens if they asked, so I'm sure there's going to be some sort of cover-up."

She snorted. "Yes, President Yang is a completely different woman around mother and Titania, isn't she?"

"The word besotted comes to mind."

She nodded and supplied, "I'd almost think they had glamoured her if it weren't for the fact I can't feel any magic emanating from her except her own."

I sat up straighter. "Wait, what? President Yang has her own magic?"

Rory chuckled at my reaction. "Of course silly, she's half-Elf, and Elves are magic. All elves can manifest magic to some extent, but most are limited to embedding it into runes or objects. The most powerful Elf is only as powerful as the youngest of the Fae."

Oh.

I shook my head then I shared, "I knew that Elves were 'born of magic' but I never knew what that meant. And I guess I should have put two and two together since elvish runes are everywhere, and they do help in the Magi-Tech industry. I've never really thought much of it since magic is such a part of life here on the world, and when you have none of your own, you never really look very deep into it."

She nodded, that slight smirk I loved to see on her lips. "And that's how most magical beings like it."

I wiggled my fingers. "Ooo... So mysterious."

She crinkled her nose.

Graz groaned from the kitchen. "Mab's tits, I'm getting cavities from way over here just watching you two," Then she whistled and her family all buzzed up to her and they left a streak of light and dust in their wake as they headed off to bed.

I grinned at our sudden privacy and her sitting so close, her scent enveloping me was driving my libido like a freight carrier. I leaned in just to find her finger on my lips, frosted steam drifted up making miniature snowflakes where Titania's mark interacted with Aurora's own icy magic. She shook her head coyly and said, "You missed your chance when you brought my mother up in an intimate moment, lady. Now you're going to have to work for it."

She stood, and smoothed her gown, looking supremely pleased with herself. She sauntered to the door as I sputtered, trying to find words to convince her to stay. The cold water of disappointment was thrown on my arousal as she snickered at the look on my face as I joined her at the door.

Rory brushed my cheek with the back of her hand and said, "See you tomorrow? Dinner? Hopefully, you'll have the case closed by then."

I nodded and she opened the door and leaned in to give me the lightest of kisses, our lips barely brushing, the fire and ice sizzling gently.

Then she was gone, and I was left there, holding the door, eyes blinking and lips parted in want. By the gods, I needed a cold shower or I was going to melt from the heat inside me. A moment later I was chuckling when her muffled voice called through the door, "And stop calling Commander Udriel."

Mother took the opportunity to show that privacy was just an abstract concept on a living ship like her. Smooth Operator by an artist named Sade started to play in the space. I muttered to the nearest camera, "Nice."

"Just a little mood music for you, Knith."

"Yuck it up, Mother, you should be a comedian."

She bantered right back. "With moves like that, I have a better chance at courting the princess."

I'd have argued the point, but Mother hadn't been the one to bring up Mab when things were starting to heat up.

I trudged back into my bedchamber, two things on my mind. Cold shower and sleep. I just ignored the slow clapping coming from the nightstand. Mab's tits, just kill me now.

CHAPTER 10
Ballroom Blitz

The next morning, I was feeling surprisingly rested. And was streaming the facts of the case on my wrist console as I ate breakfast. It was like I was looking at it with new eyes and had Mother feeding more information on all the aspects of the case.

I knew what my next move was, and Mother and Aurora were going to hate it. I cringed when I asked, "Mother, I'm going to need access to a vehicle with EVA capability."

She warned, "Knith..."

I shook my head, "I'd just go out the airlock there if it weren't damaged, and I've only got thirty minutes of air in my armor."

"Knith..."

I grinned at the ceiling camera as I patted the bulkhead lovingly, "Come on, Mother, I'll get you a World's Best Ship coffee mug for your desk."

She harrumphed, not having a desk nor being able to drink coffee. But the snarky tone she used when she said, "Requesting a vessel now," had me blurting, "No! You didn't."

She chuckled, "Commander Udriel was most amused at the request and will make herself available at eleven hundred hours, ship time. Where shall I have her pick you up?"

I thought about it then asked instead, following my hunch, "Not sure yet, depends on where the investigation takes us. Did you find anything in your data dive to show any animosity between the skin jockeys and the Fae Courts?"

She hmmed, sounding all too human, and said, "There's been a few cases of them butting heads, but it is the usual volatility when it comes to the External Maintenance Crew and their dealings with just about anyone with authority. There's only one thing I flagged for you that could go toward motive."

"Hit me with it."

I got up and washed my dishes then went into my room to change into my armor, placing a little plate of sliced bananas on the little ledge I put by the hole Graz and her family had bored into the drawer front of my nightstand.

There was a buzzing sound and when I stepped out from behind my changing screen in my armor, the plate was virtually scoured clean. I had to grin at the high pitched, pleased voices I heard coming from the drawer.

My quarters being in the A-Ring, there was an over abundance of fruits and vegetables in the markets since eighty percent of the population here were Fae, nineteen percent Elf, and one percent a smattering of other races... oh, and one human thank you very much. So I had quite a lot of fruits and veggies in my kitchen as Fae don't eat meat.

There was an Elvish butcher shop just a stone's throw away from the spoke terminal structures where my quarters were. In the lakeside town of Londeithel by the Forest of Evening Shadow, where this stack's Wood Elves lived. It was just about the only place I could get meat up here, without having to venture down-ring for a decent steak. An Elven friend of mine, J'real Leafwalker of House Thule of the Elves... it was surreal that a prince of elves was my friend now, shared the butcher shop location with me.

J'real, or Jay as his friends call him, shamelessly competes with me for Aurora's hand, I'd be jealous if he didn't flirt relentlessly with me and Rory's personal assistant, Nyx, as well. As my girl puts it, "He's a helpless flirt." By the lords of the cosmos, I'd just called Rory my girl, and I'm grinning like a loon about it.

I placed my helmet on so I could get a heads up view of the information Mother was sharing with me instead of looking down at my wrist console. I loved the enhanced heads up of my new armor as opposed to the limited heads up my old armor had. Since there was a neural interface with this new helmet, it was as if my visual space had been multiplied, and multiple displays could be shown just beyond where my normal peripheral vision should have stopped, and it was crystal clear there, like it were directly in front of me.

I'm told that if I got a data port or com jack implant, the capabilities of the helmet went up exponentially, but for some reason I'm reticent to do that. I know it is silly, but I pride myself on being one hundred percent unmodded human. I'm what they call a double-aught. Zero augments, zero cybernetic implants.

But now I know I'm about as modded as it is possible to be, at least genetically since my genetic makeup was designed from the ground up by none other than my girlfriend. It still doesn't quite compute in my head that she is over five thousand years old.

I furrowed my brow at the information Mother was showing me. It seems that this year's government budget proposals included a request for more funding for the External Maintenance Crew modernization and salary increase for the lifers to compensate for inflation.

It had been put in by Max, along with a detailed proposal to update the External Maintenance systems and procedures which haven't changed since Exodus. It was a hide bound agency like so many others that haven't kept up with modern day evolution and overhauls of shipboard operations.

He suggested that it would increase efficiency and morale of the workers, and stem turnover if they had additional funds in their budget to hire more permanent workers so they didn't have to do so much overtime or hire so many day workers.

I cocked an eyebrow, it seemed to be a no brainer to me. Max had already streamlined his stack, imagine what he could do with the proper budget for all the stacks. He made a hell of a lot of sense, and his budget request wasn't out of line or astronomical compared to some of the administration raises that were submitted from other departments.

Then I saw what Mother was eluding to as possible motive. The Greater Fae... the Summer Court, had requested a similar amount, just five percent more than the External Maintenance Crew request, for a water feature and pedestrian mall in Gamma-B as capital improvements to the other Stack under the control of the Summer Court.

It was a frivolous request, as it did nothing for the infrastructure or management of the world. It would just make the upper rings even more elite, separating the races and classes just a bit more by giving their upper class citizens yet another beautiful space to add to their paradises.

Then, as one would suspect, bowing to the Fae and not wanting to make any waves, the budget committees approved the Fae request while denying Max's since they didn't have the budget to do both. The tragedy of it was that instead of increasing the External Maintenance Crew salaries, they reduced them to absorb the five percent capital they needed to grant the Fae's budget request.

So not only did Max not get the improvements, now they were getting paid less, the workers had to do more, since the budget for day workers decreased as well by the same percentage. While the people who take the risks out in hard vacuum, maintain the Skin for everyone on the world, construction on the water feature and pedestrian mall have just finished up in Gamma-B.

That was the definition of unfair. And as much as I fault them for it, it was how our society worked here on the Leviathan. The Fae are basically in charge by proxy, since without them, the Worldship would not be possible. Though every square inch of the

hull was covered in photovoltaic paint that harvested every photon
and even cosmic radiation from the stars at ninety-eight percent
efficiency, and the fission reactors run with a dwindling fissionable
fuel supply from the rare metals mined from the Heart. They supply
a fraction of the power it takes to run the Leviathan.

Most of the energy to run the core systems and the massive
World-Drives comes from the Fae. Specifically the Fae artifacts of
power, the source of all their magic away from the Earth. Power so
vast it is difficult to comprehend. And only the Greater Fae Lords
and Ladies, under the orders of Queen Mab herself, can extract the
power safely in the Chamber of the Artifacts, the Ka'Ifinitum.

So even though we have a president, and are a democracy, and
the Fae pretend to be governed by the laws of the world... they are
the ones with the true power. And if the Fae feel slighted in any
way, things on the world, in the Rings where the ones who slighted
them live, start to mysteriously malfunction... Air scrubbers,
temperature and environmental controls, hells, even the Day Lights
or hot water generators.

So while rationally I know why the budget committee did what
they did, I still don't believe the Fae should hold that much power
over our government. And as the Fae have virtually infinite wealth
and could have done their improvements themselves, they used
government funds for their little home improvement project.

I was a little sad that my hunch was playing out here. I thought
that some skin jockeys may have had some sort of grudge against

the Summer Lady. The loose threads were, one, how did they even know about Ember, and two, how did she get outside the world to begin with?

Sighing, I said as I headed to the door, stuffing an apple in one of my belt pouches along the way, "Time to shake some trees and see what falls out. Append the files to the investigation notes so Reise doesn't call for an update?"

Mother chirped, "Already did." I had to smile, we made such a good team.

I almost jumped when Graz said from beside my head, "We gonna bust some heads?"

My visor snapped shut as fast as I could think it, before she could zip in. Her preternatural reflexes had her stopping a hair's breadth from splatting against it. She eyeballed me, squeezing one eye shut as she perched on my shoulder as I said, "No 'we' aren't doing anything. I'm going to do my job, and you're going to do whatever it is you do."

I qualified quickly, "As long as it isn't illegal."

She grumped, "You take the fun out of everything. I haven't been able to get a decent... salvage... in weeks since we moved in with you."

"Stealing is not salvage."

"You can't prove I steal anything."

"I caught you doing it the day we met."

"Semantics."

Exhaling slowly I said patiently, "Like I said before. You are a civilian. I am an Enforcer. What I do is dangerous and you don't even have permission to do a ride-along."

She tapped her tiny wrist console then clanked it against my visor. "Do now."

I blinked and my visor magnified her screen. Mother Fairy Humper! I blurted, "A private investigator license? And an undated ride along waiver? How did you get..."

I looked up, "Mother?"

She wasn't even repentant, "It was either that, press, or government office for her to qualify for a ride along permit."

"Why did you do it to begin with?"

"She asked."

"So you forged a license?"

"Artistically issued one. And besides, how do you know she doesn't qualify?"

I sputtered, "Does everyone I know play fast and loose with the law?"

Their silence was all the answer I needed. I huffed as I stepped outside, growling, "Both of you are incorrigible!"

I opened my visor to let Graz zip in before mounting up on my Tac-Bike since I knew I wasn't getting rid of her now, and she needed the protection at the speeds the bike traveled.

Graz said "That's the spirit," as Mother said cheekily, "Thank you."

"It wasn't a compliment. It was... ah, forget it, I'm not going to win."

Again Graz chirped out, "That's the spirit!"

"Smartass." Then I added as I closed the visor and we shot off toward the spoke to head down-ring. "Mother, besides the Firewyrm pens we have identified, how many other spaces are you not allowed to observe or scan?"

She seemed put out that she couldn't even scan the pens, let alone had even known they have existed, so she started with, "That I'm aware of..." Then she gave a short list, "The palaces of the Seelie and Unseelie Courts, and the Ka'Ifinitum. In addition, any judge can request privacy mode in their chambers, and the President can request privacy mode wherever she is."

Graz asked, "What does that have to do with the case? You think the arsonist will strike again?"

I smirked, "No that was for personal reasons. Just seeing how many places Rory could have stuck her mother. Of that list, it can be only one of two places, and I have a hunch."

She chirped in an ironic tone, "You always have a hunch."

"They usually prove out."

Mother mumbled, "That's what I'm afraid of."

I stole Graz's line, "That's the spirit!"

The Sprite tittered, "For a big, you're ok." Then she prompted, "So... where are we heading?"

"Going back to External Maintenance on Alpha. I need to check something before I walk the Skin."

We arrived at the scrapyard in front of External Maintenance. The huge scales of skin were set up in stacks, making corridors between the piles of other junk cleaned up from impact sites. This was a scrapper's dream. But just like almost every scrapyard on the world, all the material belonged to the ship. It would be recycled as materials were needed. Even the servos, connectors, contacts and circuitry embedded in the scrap.

So technically scrapping was illegal, but most Enforcers and agencies like this looked the other way as long as it wasn't endangering anyone. Sometimes the meager chits they could get for the junk they sell is all that keeps them off the streets and helps to feed their families better than the monthly meal ration cards everyone on the world received to ensure minimum nutrition.

Instead of heading in I asked Graz, "How can we find the newest additions to the scrap heaps?"

She just pointed, "Over there. Can't you see it?"

Mother said, "She is correct."

I asked, "See what?"

As she flew out in front of me, the flying nuisance looked back, her face contorted to one of pity, "You nulls really are almost blind, aren't you?" She pointed again, "Those over there were out in space most recently."

How did she... I had my visor rise and said, "Full spectrum." The world turned into a rainbow hued world, and then I saw it, but

Firewyrm   157

not in the infrared as I had anticipated. I wasn't sure what spectrum
I was looking at without asking, but all the junk in the heaps and
stacks had varying hues of silver emanating from them. The ones
Graz was buzzing up to were brighter silver underlying the cold
infrared emanations.

Then I got it. "Radiation signatures." My eyes widened, "You
can see that?"

Both of them answered plainly, "Yes."

I squinted an eye in apology for some reason and asked,
"Exposure to cosmic radiation burning off?" Their lack of answer
told me I was likely mostly correct.

We went up to the huge panels. All of which had varying degrees
of scorching, pitting, or in some cases, outright holes torn into them.
There were ten possible sections but none of them had the blackened
scorching I had seen. And by the relative size of each scale, I'd have
to say that three to five panels had to be replaced to hide the damage
on the Skin.

I sighed and said, "None of these is from that area. Is there a
way to tell where each of these was removed from on the Skin?"

Mother said, "Each has a micro-etched serial number, and each
is in the maintenance database to track batches and implementations
on the hull."

I sighed and said, "Odds are they just spaced them or they
haven't been offloaded from the tug or rigs yet."

Graz nodded and pointed to the far end of the yard, "Or they already sent them through the shredder/recycler."

This got my attention. She explained as she flew backwards, leading me that direction, "When they need let's say more exotherium mesh for new panels when inventory gets low, they send the scrap through the shredder. It separates all the materials into separate bins for reclamation and recycling to make new panels."

"How do you know all of this?"

She said with a shit eating grin, "Private Investigator." I sighed and she deflated and said, "Hypothetically, if say a scrapper were looking for readily sorted relays or contacts, they might just bypass the manual labor of procuring them themselves, and just help themselves to the sorting bins instead."

I cocked an eyebrow, "Hypothetically, that scrapper would be arrested since it is illegal... and that would make them a lazy thief."

She nodded and repeated cheerily, "Hypothetically." Then she brightened, "Hey look, there are some newer panels in the queue for shredding."

I looked at them and sure enough they were glowing bright in that silver spectrum. We examined them. "Mother, can you scan the micro-etching and determine if they are from the area above the pen?"

She hmmed for a moment and was silent then hmmed again. "The serial numbers are not in the database... just a moment... they seem to be connected with an encoded file in the maintenance records tagged for external maintenance management eyes only if the area around the airlock in question is ever hit."

"Can you decrypt?"

"Can I decrypt? Of course I can decrypt. But not for you Knith, even if I wanted to. They are tagged with Double Black protocol. I could show you the contents only if you have the release codes, and even then it would be for display only and my logging system would not be able to log the contents."

"Double Black? I've heard rumors of contingency protocols like that before, but nobody has ever used one. They're for like catastrophic events only. Only the president and the Queens have that clearance and anyone they tag the files as readable to. I thought that was all just made up."

I could imagine her shaking her head, "They are real, and I wouldn't be able to tell you if any have ever been used since it wouldn't be logged in my memory." She seemed put out that there were things inside of her that were hidden from her, even in her own mind.

That had me musing out loud, "What could be in a file for the external maintenance crew managers that could possibly be Double Black?"

Then I saw it. "This panel isn't like the others." I looked between the panels laying against each other then grabbed the gap between two and strained, the servos in my armor maxing out as the panels groaned and slowly moved apart enough I could see that one of them had a large rectangular hole and what looked to be the remains of an airlock seal hanging on a retracted airlock door.

"Bingo. That's how Ember got out. And as the airlock door is open and not melted through, someone had to have let her out. We have opportunity and we have motive, we just need a who."

I talked it through as I took the time to study the panels and the scorching so that Mother would record the evidence with my visual record. "Who would have access to the vessels, logs and the database records to be able to alter them to not show the repair of the area?"

She verified my thoughts, "Any of the four Stack managers, any of the fulltime salaried workers, but none of the day workers."

I prompted, "So that would give us a pool of suspects how big?"

"One thousand and four."

"Alpha-Stack only?"

"Two hundred and fifty one."

"Cross reference employees yesterday who flew out of this hangar, visual records."

"Thirty three."

I rubbed my gauntlets together and grinned, "Now we're getting somewhere. How many flights?"

She sighed. The AI actually sighed at me, "Yes yes, you're clever Knith. The answer you are whittling down to are two flights that do not have corresponding flight logs. So six suspects."

"Now we're cooking. Please pull the jackets on the six for me, now I just need to get a look again at that area on the Skin now that I know what I'm looking for... a hidden airlock." I couldn't shake the feeling I was forgetting something, but I'm sure I'd remember before this was all over.

Then I almost strutted toward the office, "Shall we go make some noise, girls?"

Graz was all smiles and Mother played Ballroom Blitz by a group called Sweet from the anthropological records.

CHAPTER 11
Dancing On the Ceiling

$\mathbf{M}$ax was asleep at his desk again, and I had sympathy for the man, knowing just how hard his schedule was and how much work he put in to streamline his department on top of it.

Spike saw us come in and poked his head up from his little bed then whimpered when Graz gave a toothy grin. That woke Max. He blinked then sat up. His smile was genuine. "Knith! What brings you back? Have you made any progress on your investigation? There's been a lack of information as the news waves are following another Enforcer, a big Grindle, I forget the name, as he forges ahead. Is he your partner?"

Doh! I almost slapped my own forehead. I'm still not used to having a partner. And I had just ditched him again this morning inadvertently. I nodded, "Lieutenant Keller."

"Yeah, that's it. Here." He made a hand motion and a screen bloomed on the wall by his desk, Eileen Brightleaf and Leviathan Network News crews were out in... was that Delta-Stack? And Daniel was feeding them all sorts of assurances that we were progressing swiftly on the case, and then a bunch of official sounding nonsense about what we were doing.

I realized that where I forget that I have a partner, he didn't. He was drawing them away from me on purpose, leaving me free and unencumbered to run the real investigation. I owed the man a fruit basket... and an apology.

I thought, "Mother?"

She replied in my head through the helmet interface, "I've already coordinated with him for you this morning, asking him to draw off the attention while you followed your hunch. Possibly in your voice."

"I love you."

"Of course you do, what's not to love?"

I asked him, not telling the full truth, "I was wanting to speak with two of your crews just to be thorough, about anything they may have seen around the fire site and the damaged Airlock that has the repair dome."

He nodded, "Of course. Though we didn't have anyone in that area, but a crew passing by may have seen something. Are you wrapping things up now?"

I nodded back, "Just dotting my I's and crossing my T's. Only need to speak with..." Mother scrolled the information to me, "Alpha Zero Seven and Alpha One Three. Then I just have to go out to look at the damage when my ride can get to me. It's all looking accidental." Unlike the Fae, I could lie real good.

He typed something on a virtual keyboard then said, "Zero seven just left on a trunk repair, and thirteen should be landing in the next hour or so. I can have one of the crews take you out on a tug to check the area out if you don't want to wait for your ride."

This man was probably the most helpful bureaucrat I've ever had to deal with. I was just sorry that I'd be binding one of his crews by law when this was all over with. "That would be great, Max, if it doesn't interrupt the work schedule. I know you're already spread thin here."

He waved it off, "Hey, as I said, we're both civil servants here, Knith, I'm sure you're no stranger to long hours and hard work."

We exchanged deranged smiles then chuckled. The man was the type you'd knock a few brews back with as you shoot the shit. When all of this was over, I was thinking about inviting him to the weekly card game on the Underhill with Mac and the crew.

He led us back into the bay, Spike keeping a wary eye on Graz, who swung two fingers from her eyes toward the dog. Max let out a shrill whistle and that crew who looked familiar to me, turned from where they were preparing one of the tugs that were equipped with two claw-like arms that were used to move around the giant scales.

One of them came jogging over in the long bounds of someone used to moving quickly in the reduced gravity down here in the D-Ring, exo-assist braces on his legs and back making his strides more powerful. "Deep, I need your crew to take the enforcer here out to do a EVA reconnoiter around the fire area up on B."

The man looked unnervingly familiar to me as he just looked me up and down, that slight imbalance which most skin jockeys had in their eyes shone brightly in his. He looked at Max like he were asking him to spontaneously turn into a bunny or something. "You sure boss?"

"Just take her where she wants to go. Keep your crazy to yourself, Deep End."

The guy flipped off his supervisor then did a curtsy to me, making a sweeping ushering motion, "After you, enforcer."

I rolled my eyes and held out a fist, Max bumped it and said, "Ow."

I looked at my armored hand, "Oops, sorry. This won't take long, I promise."

The guy Max called Deep End said, "Today sometime would be nice, princess."

I sighed then covered the distance in four bounds, arriving at the tug just before him. He cocked an eyebrow. "Pretty comfortable in reduced G for an up-ringer."

I let him keep his air of superiority since they were doing me a favor. I pointed at my chest, "Enforcer armor."

He grinned, accepting the lie, since in his head, I couldn't possibly have beat him. I was just at home in any gravity since I have trained for decades for combat and emergency situations in zero G, micro gravity, and enhanced gravity like the A-Rings. I didn't need my armor to navigate quickly down here.

I looked at the big guy with his shaved head, he looked so familiar. He saw me looking and he smiled, not in a friendly way, and most of his front teeth gleamed of metal. Why hadn't he just had new ones grown for him instead? Then I remembered what I had just learned about their pay and realized he probably couldn't afford new teeth, especially because I could see the tell tale bulge of a med tech bio-pack under his shirt. He's had cybernetic organ replacement, again not being able to afford new ones just being grown for him.

He said as we paced up the ramp, which doubled as a door, up into the belly of the tug. At least here is one place the government didn't cut corners, the skin jockey tugs may not look pretty, but they were beasts of burden that were almost indestructible. Their top of the line, industrial robotic arms made them look like mechanical monsters.

There were two smaller craft, maintenance rigs, that looked like miniature versions of the ship, just grafted to an EVA suit and heavy loader exoskeleton with magnetic treads and mini thrusters to keep them in contact with the Skin, as well as two additional, standard issue EVA suits with twenty four hour air supplies were secured beside the rigs.

The center of the bay had racks that held three of those immense Skin panels, and on the opposite wall were racks full of parts, tools, and even a diagnostic rack. These tugs were impressive smaller cousins of the maneuvering assist tugs that helped in the Turnover Event when I was a little kid.

Two other skin jockeys turned around from where they were securing a panel. The lanky woman froze for a moment then stood up straight, eyes narrowing. Besides the exo-assist braces on her legs and back, she looked to be unmodded.

The other man had one cut rate cybernetic eye, I could read the electromagnetic signature from it as old fashioned infrared beams swept over me to feed data to the iris to focus on me. He didn't look any friendlier than the other two.

Deep End held up a hand, like he was stalling them. "Legs, Gripper, the boss wants us to give Enforcer Shade here a ride outside. We're happy to, aren't we?" How did he know my name? Max hadn't said it.

They furrowed their brows then started to smile. Legs said in a raspy tone, "Of course."

Then she elbowed Gripper when his brow furrowed even farther, almost swallowing his eyes completely. "Oh... yeah."

Deep End told me as he leapt over me, and landed on the catwalk ten feet above, then up another level to go into the cockpit, "Better strap in up here. Maintenance tugs aren't as smooth as your fancy up-ring vehicles."

I sighed and followed suit. I had a four to five foot vertical leap unassisted in the light gravity down here, so my armor servos gave me the additional boost to mirror his moves. They likely could have flung me the entire distance but I didn't want to try and fail in front of this cheery bunch.

The other jockeys followed, Legs saying as she looked at my armor as she landed beside me, "Well alright." She pushed past me, Gripper doing the same.

We stepped through a small airlock onto the bridge. It felt a little cramped with the four of us, but it did have seating for six. They were already strapping in with obvious ease of someone who has done it for years as Deep End started spinning up the plasma drives. I heard the ramp door clang into place below us.

Oh space me naked, he wasn't going to wait! I sat in a seat across from the other two, and fumbled with five point strap linkage. Graz was wrapping her arms in my hair as she said with urgency, "Umm, Knith?"

I muttered, "I know," as I activated my mag boots just in case but slammed the buckles home just as the ship lurched and swung around fast enough to make me want to re-visit my recent eating choices. Then we were lunging forward toward the closing inner bay doors.

Didn't he see they were closing for another tug already? I grabbed the arms of the chair, and heard metal groaning in protest as it started to bend under my grip. And we slid through the opening with just inches to spare.

We came to a hovering halt beside another tug and when the warning lights signifying hard vacuum started flashing and the outer door cycled open, Deep End slammed the controls forward and we shot out of the bay like the hounds of Faerie were on our tail.

Then the man was calling out over his shoulder, "B-Ring fire area, enforcer?"

I nodded, "Yes, please. I appreciate the ride."

I looked to the others, "Legs? Gripper?"

The woman said as she took off her heavy leather gloves and flexed her fingers, "He runs the tug's arms. I'm the EVA specialist with the Rigs." Ahh, I thought she was Legs because she was so lanky, but it was more practical than that. I didn't want to ask about what Deep End's name meant then.

I hesitated when I saw her rubbing her palm where the flesh ended in a diagonal line and cybernetic replacements for the other half of her palm and her four fingers began. I tried to not react as I realized why this crew looked so familiar. They were the skin jockeys Lord Sindri had sent to kill me in the back corridors of the Underhill. All of their new cyber-gear was courtesy of the beating I and Mir gave them.

They must have transferred to the Alpha stack after the incident in case I came looking for them. But as much as I would have liked to, they had attacked me on a Remnant vessel, thus outside the laws of the world, so I couldn't.

I tried to act nonchalant, "So that would make Deep End...?"

She snorted, "He's just fuckin' nuts."

We sat in an awkward silence after that, them watching me with amused malice, until Deep End called back. "We're here. Setting down next to the repair dome. Legs, why don't you take our guest down and help her into an EVA suit."

Yeah, no way in hell that was happening. I can see it accidentally having an unfortunate catastrophic malfunction. Mother was in my head, "Knith, is everything ok? Your heart rate has increased alarmingly, like it does when you're fighting."

I thought, "Not now." I couldn't exactly tell her who these people were over the helmet's neuro interface, it could only pick up surface thoughts, not detailed explanations. She made an affirmative sound.

As I unbuckled myself and stood quickly, my mag-boots holding me to the deck as I moved quickly to the little airlock, I said, "No need, just drop the ramp for a girl?"

I hit the door control, cycling it closed in Legs and Gripper's faces as my visor raised. And before they could re-cycle it I hit the decompression buttons for the airlock and bay beyond. My armor reconfigured to emergency EVA mode. A thirty minute oxygen timer started in my heads up display as Deep End said over coms, "What are you doing, Shade? Are you insane?"

I said, "No, I'm fine. This isn't standard Enforcer armor. And I won't need a ride back, I've got a ride. Thanks."

I had to take the stairs down each level, as I heard the bay starting to repressurize. They were going to come after me. I clomped over to the door controls and said, "Mother? Open the bay doors. Override authorization, Brigade zero four."

With the woosh of depressurization of what little air they had already started pumping back in, the hard vacuum light started flashing again and I stepped onto the ramp and clunked my way down until I stood on the Skin. Only then did my brain catch up to me. Mab's tits, was I crazy? I was outside in the hard vacuum of space!

The door raised and Deep End pinged my coms, "Ok, you crazy Enforcer, I sure hope you know what you're doing." Then the Tug flew up just missing me as they took off up toward the A-Ring.

I just stood there a moment until Graz said, "Flat out crazy. Of all the nulls on the world, I get stuck with the one with a death wish." Then she addressed me directly, "You stupid big!"

I nodded, unable to disagree as I whispered, "Pretty much," as I stared up into the blackness between the Stacks to the nebula, shining in all its glory to remind me just how small and insignificant I was. I swallowed and whispered, "Mother?"

She sounded amused as she said, "Commander Udriel has been informed and will be here for pickup before you finish your inspection."

I nodded and right on cue, Myra was on coms. I sighed and accepted it. She offered no pleasantries, "You're certifiable Shade."

I whispered, "That's the general consensus circulating here."

She whispered back, "Why are we whispering?"

I hadn't realized I had been until then. I said normally, half in question with a little waver in my tone, "I just felt that I didn't want the universe to notice me out here, with only my Enforcer armor between me and oblivion?"

"Valid answer, carry on."

I snorted and she added, "Just ping me when you're about done and I can be there in two."

I nodded and Mother said mechanically, "Lieutenant Shade is nodding in the affirmative."

"Weirdo."

"Ten four. I'll ping you."

Then I closed the channel and looked past the dome to the area I needed to look at more closely. "Something appropriate please Mother?"

A tune called Dancing On The Ceiling by a man called Lionel Richie started to play, causing me to snort as I bopped to the beat. "Well ok... but we need to work on your humor." If a computer can stick its tongue out at you, her silence accomplished it. See? Redheads.

I clomped along with only the lights from the Day Lights of the A-Ring above me, and the nebula illuminating the metallic charcoal grey of the skin, my mag boots the only thing stopping me from being flung off the rotating ring into deep space.

"Can you..."

"Scanning the micro-etched serial numbers as you walk, Knith, if the numbering is consistent, it is the next scale."

Twenty more steps of my slow progress and she said, "This is it." I nodded and asked, "Do I have power for lights?"

Graz answered for her, "Power isn't the problem, air is." Duh, I should have known that. With a thought, powerful beams of light at the sides of my helmet cut through the dark to illuminate the hull, I could see the micro pulses of energy generation from the

photovoltaic paint which covered the Leviathan reconverting the
light to power for the world.

I envisioned the panel I had seen and took three long strides
forward and saw an almost invisible seam. I paced it off and it was
the same size as the jammed airlock from the scrap heap. I slowly
walked the seam until I saw what I was looking for and crouched
and pushed a small panel and it slid down, then in, revealing a small
set of airlock controls.

I said, "This is the place. Shall we?"

I ignored the chorus of no's as I cycled the airlock and after it
showed negative pressure inside, the door slid down the opening,
revealing a smaller than standard airlock. I grabbed the hand holds
of the zero-G grip bars and swung myself in, and climbed what felt
like up in my new orientation and cycled the door. I sighed in relief
and stood on the door then hit the second control, and after a
moment external sound started to return as I heard the hissing of the
compartment pressurizing.

Then the door opened. I smiled and went up the short ladder as
my armor reconverted to normal, my visor flicking up and the micro
pumps in my suit recharging my air supply for later. I pulled myself
up to stand in...

My jaw must have hit the ground as the door closed after us,
because we were definitely not in a large pen for a scared animal.
As far as my eyes could see was rocky terrain with lush forests and
streams and waterfalls. Were these... were these mountains?

I could smell air rich with plants and water, but my eyes couldn't completely focus on the amazing landscape that lay before me. I realized as I whispered, "It's magic. This place is saturated with a glamour so powerful I can't completely see through it. They've created a world for Ember... a gilded cage instead of a metal and ceramic box."

Graz buzzed out and down to some flowing moss I was standing on. She said in awe, "This looks like the Jotunheim Mountain range in Scandinavia."

I blinked at the sight before me, then down to her. She eludes to being old all the time, and Sprites, though possessing limited immortality, usually meet with violent ends early on in life. So not many old ones, who remember the Earth that was, remained. This is the first time she had inadvertently verified that she was one of the ancient ones of her race. Then again, they did protect their pollinators, as they were extremely rare in the tri-sexual species, so her survival was paramount to them.

Was this what open air was like? Someone nudged my leg as we looked off across the mountains. I glanced over and said, "Hi Ember," and started to look back toward the amazing illusion in front of us before doing a double take and almost falling on my ass, but my armor's internal gyros stabilized me.

There standing beside us was the huge Firewyrm, looking far too cute for something so immense and dangerous, her eyes on my hip. I looked from her to my hip then grinned. I pulled out the apple from one of my belt packs, asking, "Is this what you want, girl?"

Her immense tail swished, sparking the air behind her with unbridled magic flame. I held a hand out, retracting the nano-panels, and she moved forward, letting me place my hand on her immense muzzle. Her silverish hair was soft as down, and it heated up as it was stroked, magic pouring out from the contact.

I whispered in awe, "You are so beautiful. Here you go, Ember." I gave her the apple. She happily crunched it between her massive fangs and swallowed. Nudging me again. I chuckled and laid my forehead against her. "That's the only one I have. I'll bring you more sometime, ok? I promise."

Flashes of images and feelings came from her. She was pleased and I had to smile at her. I realized Graz was plastered to the back of my calf and I looked back at her, her eyes bulging wide. I said, "Oh get up here, scaredy-cat. She won't hurt you."

Graz looked at me dubiously then buzzed up to sit on my hand as I held her out in front of Ember's saucer sized eyes. She started to open her mouth and I chuckled at the squeak of distress from Graz as I said, "No, she's not for eating. She's a friend. Like you and me."

She brought a huge nostril to my hand and sniffed, Graz was screaming and holding onto my thumb to stop from getting sucked in. I caught a flash of amazement, then the impression of the word friend. Then I nudged my eyes at the Sprite. She huffed then turned to the dragon, "Um, hi? Nice to meet you? I'm Graz? We met before."

Then her eyes widened as I felt the impression of those flashes of communication seemed to pass between them. Then Graz smiled hugely and patted Ember's nostril. "You're ok, Ember."

I said, "See? There's nothing to be afraid of here."

A voice beside me said, as Titania peered down my arm at Graz, "I wouldn't say that... human."

Then she was gone and fifteen feet away from us and Ember lit up... literally. Her excitement driving her magic flame and heating up the area, sending Graz screaming as she buzzed up and dove into my armor. Ember was bouncing like an excited child as she coiled around the Summer Lady and they seemed to commune in a mini-inferno that had my visor sliding up and my armor reconfiguring to fire mode.

Then as the flames started to die back down, Queen Titania stepped through the flames, appearing by all measures to be a goddess of fire, to look me up and down as my visor opened again. "You're more resourceful than I had imagined. I take it you're here to give me the party responsible for terrorizing my baby here?"

I squinted one eye as if in pain, "Not exactly. I needed to determine how Ember was let out to begin with, without tripping your wards, since I don't believe Mab had anything to do with it. And here I am, a human with no magic, inside Ember's pen. If you wouldn't have been so evasive and secretive, I wouldn't have had to do this. I have some solid leads now."

She looked from me to the space on the moss where the airlock door was supposed to be. I could see a shimmer through the magic as I tried to focus beneath the illusion. She said, "Yes, I'll have to make sure to ward that entry point too. We never would have thought anyone would ever use it."

Then she stalked away with Ember following her, "If you don't find the guilty party by the time the Day Lights go out, you'll be adorning my receiving hall as a fruit tree. You have two minutes to get out of here before I throw you out with prejudice... little miss nobody."

She was having fun with my name, rubbing it in that Shade means Nobody in Old Faerie. Then my eyes widened. Space me naked, I had to get out of here before she made good on her promise. "Buckle up Graz."

I reconfigured to EVA mode as I patted around the magic created moss under my feet for the airlock controls. As the door opened and we fell through, Mother informed me, "I signaled Commander Udriel, she'll be here in two minutes for the extract."

Good.

Once the doors cycled after depressurization I climbed back out onto the Skin. My mag boots had just engaged when Mother yelled, "Knith, look out!" Just as what felt like a herd of charging Minotaurs hit me, sending alarms blaring in my suit and system damage warnings scrolling in my vision as I was flung off of the world, tumbling toward open space.

CHAPTER 12
The Warrior

As I spiraled out of control in a cacophony of alarms blaring, red overlays showed damage to the armor. My mind finally supplied me with the missing piece I had overlooked. I was oddly calm, spiraling up toward the gap between the A-Rings toward open space.

I had the three mercenary skin jockey's pegged for the culprits, but what had been nagging at me was that they didn't have access to the Double Black encoded files about the hidden airlock. Only a manager level maintenance clearance would unlock them. My heart sank because I genuinely liked and respected the man. I whispered to myself, "Max."

Then I shook my head and tried to concentrate. There was too much noise and lights and screens flashing at me. I shouted, "Silence alarms, minimize screens!"

Everything went silent but one alarm that was screaming shrilly, "We're gonna diiiiiiiiiiie!"

"Graz, shut up, let me think!"

She snapped her mouth shut.

I tracked our rotation. "Mother, status?"

She said with stress coloring her tone, "The tug hit you expertly, at the proper angle and force to send you between the stacks out into interstellar space. Power modules were damaged and you are on emergency power only. Main processors are down, you are on backups."

Ok... remember my training. Uncontrolled spin. Right. The compressed gas canisters in my packs! I touched my hip and cussed. This mode of my armor encased everything with its nano-panels. I couldn't access the canisters. Then my eyes widened. "Mother, can you take over control of the suit's nano-panel systems?"

"Yes, but..." She caught my train of thought. "That's brilliant!" Then she added, "The Commander is on afterburner, ETA seventy-three seconds. This will use thirty-seven percent of your oxygen reserves."

Then I could feel small holes opening up in the suit in an orchestrated pattern that sent streams of air out of the suit until my spin stabilized and my rotation arrested. Ok, now I could focus! I looked down to see us moving away from the Tug on the skin at a fast rate. The number A13 was emblazoned on the roof of the vehicle which confirmed Deep End's crew were one of the two I had suspected, and they hadn't been out like Max had said.

Graz was babbling in a panic, "She can't stop our momentum like that, there isn't enough air for that. Knith, what do we do?"

I had an idea and reached for my hip again and cursed. I couldn't get to my pouches, I had already determined that. If I survived this, I'd have to talk to the R&D department to fix that oversight. Again I asked, "Mother, can you access my gear?"

"What do you need?" She sounded like she was about to pass out.

"Can you put one of the mag-bands on lockdown momentarily?"

She actually gasped and said, "Affirmative, hang on, this might hurt."

I almost got whiplash as I was suddenly jerked downward from my waist, and then we were speeding down toward the Skin again.

Graz said as she climbed up to my cheek, pulling herself hand over hand, her voice filled with concern, "Umm, Knith?"

I muttered, "I know, I know. Hang on!" I activated my mag boots and prepared myself. We hit like a missile, my armor's servos taking the brunt of the impact, normally I would have rolled to absorb most of the impact, but I couldn't outside the world or I'd get flung back off, so my legs took the rest of the impact as servo motors shorted. I grunted, refusing to yell in pain. Then it was over and I stood on shaky legs. The nano-panels reconfigured as I took an experimental step without leg servo assist. The armor was light and re-conformed around me as I moved under muscle power only.

I think both legs were fractured though, if the pain was any indication. Graz was again saying, "Umm, Knith?"

I looked at the Tug as its ramp lowered and two jockey rigs rolled out, speeding my way, quickly covering the hundred and fifty yards which separated us. I sighed, cracked my knuckles and rolled my head on my shoulders as I said, "Round two. Mother? Something appropriate please?"

All my camera feeds bloomed in my peripheral, giving me a
three hundred and sixty-degree view as I started charging at the
incoming skin jockeys. I tore a ranging antenna off the skin while I
ran, wielding it like a bow-staff as The Warrior by Scandal blasted in
the helmet in time with my heartbeat.

My targeting systems were offline and I squinted as the rogue
skin jockeys approached. I could make them out through the visor
like windows. They looked like ten-foot-tall mechanical golems,
with tracks instead of legs, bearing down on me. One had a pair of
photonic fusers in the mechanical arms of the servicing rig.

Those things were used to scrape off materials on the hull and to
cut through just about any wreckage on the skin from meteorite
impacts.

The other held a fuser in one arm, and in the other, some sort of
insulated hooked pole that looked to be used to disconnect power
couplings, which it currently held like a spear. I shifted my
approach so I would clash with the dual fuser wielding rig when I
saw Gripper's face through the window.

Mother was saying, "Knith, you can't fight a Mark-3
maintenance rig, let alone two."

I said, "Not now, Mother. Things to do, people to see."

Graz told her, "She's lost it. Certifiable..."

"Zip it. Here they come."

Just a second before we clashed, I sent the mental command for
my helmet lights to pulse at two hundred percent, burning them out

in just a moment. Both the rigs raised their mechanical limbs to cover their windows as they lost track of me. That had to hurt, but they'd recover in a couple of seconds... Gripper would be worse off as the plasma burst would have burned out most of the optical receptors in his old cyber tech eye and it would take a while for it to compensate.

He'd have a huge headache after this, but not as big as if my next move hit his actual head as I ducked under the fusers he was swinging wildly and swung my improvised weapon using as much rotation as I could while keeping my feet latched to the Skin. In the silence of space, the antennae bent and tore itself apart as it struck his visor window, sending cracks spider-webbing across it.

I stepped past him, keeping the bulk of his rig between me and Legs while he dropped one fuser, leaving it drifting on its tether as he covered the worst of the spider-webbed ceramic infused plastic with the mechanical arm's hand. I saw him reaching up into the oversize helmet with an emergency molecular patch kit as I tried to reason with them on coms,

"Come on, Legs, Gripper, it doesn't have to go down like this. Right now you're only wanted for arson, nobody has been hurt yet. Stand down and consider yourself bound by law."

Deep End called out, "This is payback, Shade. I know you have to have remembered us. We certainly remember you. It's just a shame that whore from the brothel isn't here to save you this time."

Then to them, he said, "Kill the bitch."

I sighed as Gripper growled, "With pleasure, just give me a second."

One of my feet was pulled out from under me and I saw Legs had slid that hooked pole between the treads of Gripper's rig to trip me up. My other boot almost detached from the hull as I fell back. Shit! She rasped out with a chuckle, "Hurry up dolt, hold her down... I'm taking her hand before we take her out. I owe her."

I regained my footing and leapt, detaching my mag boots and grabbing the tethered fuser, using my momentum to swing around Gripper as I switched on the fuser and swung, slicing cleanly through one of Leg's mechanical arms like it wasn't even there, the fuser and arm spiraled away off into the void.

I activated my mag boots, stretching one foot down, and I was barely in range for the magnets to pull me slowly down until they engaged. I slashed backward, burying the fuser into Gripper's Rig. I could see all the flashing warning lights inside his rig as it depressurized. I closed my eyes for a second and whispered into space, "I'm sorry."

Then I tried to pull the fuser free, but it was stuck. Double shit. I backed away, grabbing a metallic piece of debris floating past, it looked to be a knuckle from one of the arms I had sliced through. Great, might as well have been a stone knife or club. I taunted, trying to sound more confident than I was, "Looks like you lost another hand there, Legs. You might want to take better care of them than that."

She screamed out in frustration and she was on top of me faster than I could backpedal. My reflexes could barely keep up as she struck at me with the pole, over and over, my arms shook with each impact and I slid back on the hull five feet or more with each strike.

Deep End was on coms, "Trisha, get the fuck out of the way and I'll just run her ass over with the tug. She's dangerous!"

I thought to myself, "No, Trish, Keep pushing your attack so he doesn't make me a splat on his windscreen."

I cut coms and asked, "Mother? Where's Myra?"

"Fifteen seconds out."

Then I screamed in pain when I deflected a down thrust, but the mechanical arm was multiple times stronger than me and her thrust didn't stop, and the armor sparked in space as the hooked end stabbed through the muscle of my left leg. Alarms were again blaring as the nano-panels formed a mostly airtight seal around the pole.

When she went to yank the pole back I went with it, like a butterfly on a pin. I opened a channel again and said through the excruciating pain, "Is that all you got?" My voice ragged and gasping.

She pulled the improvised spear to her so she could look at me as she smiled cruelly through her window. I glanced at the insulated pole, my eyes blurry with pain, then at the remains of her other mechanical arm, drizzling sparks in space.

She said, "Just wanted to say fuck you, before I killed you, bitch."

I smiled weakly and said, "I'm not so easy to kill, Trish." Then my hand shot out and grabbed the a sparking cable from the damaged arm, yanked some slack free, and jammed it into the diagnostic data port on the chest of her rig.

I heard her screams for a moment on coms before static. Deep End was yelling Trish's name as I ground out through the pain in my leg as the arm dropped and the pole dislodged from its grip, "Where's Myra?"

I looked up to see the tug's engines fire and the vessel started to careen toward me. Then it was gone in a fireball, the shock-wave and debris pelting me, damaging my armor more. I was gasping for what limited air I had left when a smug voice sounded on coms, "She's right here, Shade. You have a death wish or something?"

Graz and Mother chimed out emphatically in unison, "Yes!"

I chuckled and said as I shut down all the alarms, "If you're all done mocking me, could I possibly get a ride to Med-Tech? I seem to be leaking fluids into my boots. Some of it blood, some not."

The Ready Squadron Sentinel ship was the most beautiful sight I had ever seen as it swung around to hang millimeters off the Skin in front of me, the airlock door opening. The two steps I needed to take to get some momentum were the most painful of my life, fractures and torn up muscles before I deactivated the mag boots to drift up into the chamber. I could barely get inside with that damn pole through my leg.

Graz was buzzing out of my helmet the moment the airlock pressurized and my helmet snicked halfway up, sparking. She seemed at home in the virtual zero-G. I chuckled and muttered, "Sure, run away. I'm ok."

The moment the inner door opened, Graz was in Myra's face, speaking shrilly in a panic, "You gotta fix her! She's hurt, bad!"

I looked up from the feet which stopped in front of me. Myra looked alarmed, but she tried to play it cool. "You done fucked yourself up, Knith. Did you really just take on two Jockey Rigs hand to hand in hard vacuum? And won?"

I chuckled and looked at her helplessly. "We have different definitions of winning, you and I," motioning a hand to my sparking armor and my messed up leg.

She shook her head, whistled, then descended upon me with a plasma blade and an emergency med-kit. My eyes widened and I whimpered at the plasma blade as she lowered it to the pole. She rolled her eyes. "Wimp."

Before too long, I was strapped in the co-pilot seat as we rocketed toward a Beta-Stack Ready Squadron hangar because they had the finest doctors and Fae healers in their own Med-Bay. I had quipped, "Only the best for Ready Squadron."

"You better believe it."

Mother was in my ear. "Why do you have to keep doing this sort of thing?"

What? It wasn't like I did it on purpose.

Then I hissed in pain when Graz poked the field bandage on my leg. "Does that hurt? Good. You crazy big." Then she softened as she buzzed up to hold my nose on either side in her hands, "I'm glad you're not dead."

I nodded. "Me too."

Then I asked, "Mother?"

She sounded pleased and vindicated as she said, "A contingent of Brigade Enforcers is currently binding Commander Hardy by law." Myra cocked an eyebrow at the emotion in Mother's tone.

I nodded to myself in relief, and our Sprite companion asked, "Max? Well Titania's panties, I liked the null."

As the ship glided nimbly into the hangar, I muttered, "Me too."

CHAPTER 13

Viva La Vida

I winced for another reason the moment the med-tech medics and Fae carried me out of the ship on a litter. A very angry and concerned-looking Winter Maiden was standing there, arms crossed over her chest. Frost was building up on her and spreading across the floor at her feet. Some Knith was in trouble, and I think it was me.

She huffed and dropped her arms, ice and frost falling from her clothing as she strode up to me. The lead med-tech looked about to tell her to go wait somewhere, but he had the common sense enough to hold his tongue when a Greater Fae was approaching with her magics leaking everywhere, eyes aflame with icy fire.

Aurora looked at the shambles of my armor, some of which was fused to my skin and would likely have to be peeled off, and at my leg. Then she slapped me upside the head as I lay on the litter suspended by the two Naiad water nymph orderlies, judging by their blue hair and lips. "What were you thinking? Going out there alone without backup? You could have been..."

The med-tech said as he looked at the preliminary scans he was taking, "Lady Aurora, we need to get her to the surgical ward. Her femoral artery was torn... we don't know why she hasn't bled out yet, it looks as if something stemmed the flow. We'll need to replace a section of it with a trilon mesh, and..."

Rory huffed in frustration with her guards looming over her shoulder. "Children, you're all children. Set her there. Now." She pointed at a trauma room, the man started to argue but her eyes flared, frost seemed to cover the corridors instantly. He swallowed and motioned to the trauma room.

The orderlies complied, their eyes on Rory like they were looking at their goddess. I realized they likely thought they were since if I remembered my Naiad folklore correctly, they worshiped Acionna, the Celtic water goddess, and Queen Mab who could shape water and mold it to her will to form impossible creations in winter's ice.

The med-tech called out as I was transferred to an exam table, "We'll need a molecular de-bonder for the armor fused with her skin, a compression unit so we can remove the impaling object and..."

Aurora said, "Move back." She made a parting motion with her hands and everyone slid back like the space between them and I had just simply grown and nobody had really moved. Aurora hesitated a moment as she passed Myra, and stopped to look her in the eye before she stepped up to me and made a growing motion with her hands, pulling them apart like she held an invisible inflating ball between them.

I gasped in pain as my armor just tore away from me, hovered in the air and dropped to the ground. I squeaked out at her, "Ow!"

She paused a moment, an unrepentant look on her face as she said, "That hurt? Good. It's what you get for insisting on tilting at windmills like this. One of these times it will actually be a dragon and that will be the end of it."

Then she leaned in and whispered, "Just because you heal fast doesn't make you indestructible. I don't know why you are in such a hurry to die, and just when you learn you have the capacity to live forever."

I shrugged and said in a normal tone, "I'm sorry, but this is who I was long before we met. I can't change who I am."

She sighed and smiled, nodded, and said, "I know. And that is one of the things that has me drawn to you, Knith Shade, Enforcer of the Brigade. You've more courage than sense."

Then she leaned down and her lips brushed mine and I was in one of the heavens, forgetting about all the incessant pain and aches of my body until I was seeing stars and shouting, "Mother fairy humper!"

I had to fight to prevent the new pain in my leg from overwhelming me and to stay conscious as I looked to her hand which had the remains of the pole crushed between her sculpted ice fingernails. That reminded me again, just how insanely strong the Greater Fae were, and it terrified me for the most part, but my pain addled brain thought it was sexy as hells on Rory.

My voice rasped with the pain, "You distracted me."

The med-tech was blurting out, "What are you doing? The trauma to the tissues and... she'll bleed out in..."

She hissed at him, "Enough!" Then she looked at me, lying

naked in front of her, a mass of bruises and cuts, and burns, where the nano-panels had either ice burned into my flesh from the cold of space or burned into it from the overheated and shorting power supplies. My legs fractured, and one mangled, a pool of blood starting to soak the padded table beneath me. I felt so very small.

She started chanting in a language forgotten long before man ever walked old Earth, it built upon itself as frost swirled in the room, the temperature dropping as everything iced over, including my skin, but I didn't feel cold. Ever since Mab marked me, their icy magic didn't seem to bother me much anymore.

Her voice filled the universe, a haunting echo of a memory being pulled from all points in time, reminding me that she was her mother's daughter and almost rivaled her in power. The room was shaking as she pulled more power to her, shaping it to her will, and it gladly bowed before her.

Then she passed her hands over me, leaving me in a cocoon of translucent ice that glowed an eerie blue. Now... I was freezing. This ice was pure magic, so dense that it was sucking the heat out of the world. I would have screamed in pain as it seemed to collapse in on itself, into me, suffusing every cell in my body, burning me with its icy tendrils... but nothing came from my mouth.

Rory stopped as the pain and power seemed to just melt away. She swayed and stumbled, but Myra caught her with a hand and her tail, steadying her. I felt... well I felt wiped out, but most of the pain was gone.

I looked down to see my leg was healed, just a nasty puckering scar remained and red patches where the burns had been all over me, but I knew it would all be gone in a few days as my natural healing ability repaired me, and the bruising all over my body would fade quickly too.

Rory had helped me before, but nothing this extensive. And it tired her out because my body rejects magic so she had to pour many times more into it than she normally would. And the amount of magic she poured into this almost rivaled the power of the wards the Queens had put around their palaces.

I sat up and reached out a hand to steady her as the med-techs swarmed me, taking readings as they looked between me and her in incredulity. This was the difference between the power of a Winter Maiden and the lesser Fae Lords and Ladies who did minor healing spells for Med-Tech. "You ok, Rory? You didn't need to exhaust yourself like that, Med-Tech is good. They could have taken care of me."

She nodded, caught her breath then said, "With their archaic methods? Cutting into you, replacing parts?" Rory then offered sweetly to the medical personnel around us, "Offense not intended, I'm sure you are a credit to your profession."

Ok, I snorted at her backhanded compliment to them. But they didn't seem to even notice as they were excitedly chattering between themselves, all taking scans of me and comparing their pads. I cleared my throat. "Umm... I'm a little naked here, can I cover up?"

Graz buzzed up to me and said, "You can't be a little naked, Knith. You're full on showing your goodies. Is your brain damaged? Did she not heal that? I mean I know you bigs don't have much going on upstairs, to begin with, but..." I made a zipping motion over her lips and she shut her little yap and gave me a dirty look then turned to everyone. "Yup, she's ok."

I glared at Myra who was just grinning as she looked at me from head to toe. She held her hands up in surrender then turned to leave the room. Graz zipped up to land on her shoulder, she was babbling to her as they headed down the hall, "You're a badass coming in guns blazing. You saved our asses when you..."

Snickering I smirked. Good, Graz could annoy Myra now. I turned back to see Rory glaring at me. Gulp. "Commander Udriel? Really? What happened out there? I got the call from Mother, telling me you were out on the skin, facing down a couple of suspects in maintenance rigs." Then she paused and looked around. "My girl asked for some clothes, why are you all just standing around?" Everyone looked at her, her hair was rippling out behind her, her icy glare was literally causing ice to form on their clothes. They scurried off like rats.

Then she looked at me for answers and I just grinned sheepishly. "Mother was making a big deal about nothing. It wasn't all that bad..."

The persnickety AI took umbrage at that and the binary jerk turned on the info screen on the wall, and a news wave special report started playing. Eileen Brightleaf was outside the Alpha-Stack's External Maintenance Crew Office, an inset video was playing beside her as she was in the middle of saying, "... obtained exclusive footage of Lieutenant Knith Shade of the FABLE office of the Enforcers Brigade, engaging arson suspects connected with the inferno on Alpha-B."

The inset video expanded to take up the whole wave, and I watched from what was identified as external maintenance observation camera alpha seven ninety-three. I groaned and squinted an eye in mock pain, wishing Rory wasn't seeing this as I saw myself with the antenna in my hand, charging at the two mech-suited skin jockeys.

Maybe I WAS nuts.

She glared between the screen and me, then covered her mouth as I clashed with the huge mechanical rigs. I had to grin a little because at the time I had felt like I was moving around in a slow and clunky manner, not to mention I was scared to hells and desperate, but from a neutral observer point of view, it looked like all my luck and improvisation played out like a choreographed battle.

I winced when the hooked pole was thrust through my leg in memory of the white-hot pain of it. Then when it was over, the tug came into view as it sped toward me, just to be engulfed in a flaming explosion and power discharge, a piece of debris taking out the camera.

With a squinted eye I said, "See? Not that bad..."

While Eileen Brightleaf was talking about my injuries and how I was being rushed to medical, Rory just stared at me like I had just grown a second head.

An intern saved me by coming in with a medical smock. Rory stepped back while I donned it, cataloging the aches and pains of my healing bruises. I thanked the intern then I stood, looked around until I spotted my new armor, in a melted, twisted mess on the floor, my helmet was nowhere to be seen. Zak was going to slap me with all four arms then assign me the crappiest third-hand armor at supply for destroying the experimental next-gen armor.

I looked down at myself and sighed and said, "I guess I better get to Brigade Supply and get into proper gear before I question Max and debrief. The commander is probably suffering apoplexy since us enforcers are supposed to stay out of the spotlight, not be plastered all over the news like Daniel and I have been the past twenty-four hours. I'm sure I'll have sewage duty... or mine security again."

The med-techs were blurting out, "You can't go anywhere until you are cleared by us to return to..."

Rory held up a halting hand. "I'm still on the rosters as a level seven med-tech, and she's under my care."

A male orderly started to say, "There's no level seven, Doctor Zamir runs the department and they are level five..."

The look the lead tech was giving him had him trailing off. Did my girl's magic put her that far ahead of the department head? Then

I realized it wasn't just her magic. I fell for her intelligence as much as for how she called me on my bullshit.

She had come closer than anyone to be able to engineer a method for which the Fae could procreate this far from Earth to bring their numbers back to Equilibrium. So her raw knowledge in the medical field coupled with her healing magic earned her a rating so high.

I shuddered in realization that her half brother, Sindri, likely approached her level of competence in the field, he just lacked the one thing Aurora had... a moral core. He didn't care who he hurt... who suffered, since they were insignificant to him, just a means to an end.

Her icy glare got the dissenters in the room to back down. Then she said to me, "Are you good to move?" I nodded and she said expectantly, "Transfer her care to me."

The doc exhaled then sighed and tapped something on their pad and handed it to Rory, who pressed her thumb on it. "There, now let's get you home..."

I shook my head, knowing there was going to be an argument, and looked around to the people present. She looked around then waved a hand absently and a bubble of raw magic that looked to be a thin bubble of crystal clear ice formed around us. "They cannot hear us now."

With an apologetic look, I told her in a low tone as we watched Graz buzz around on the outside of the ice globe, looking for a way in. "We're investigating it as a simple arson as far as the rest of the people on the world are concerned since the knowledge that there are Firewyrms on board could cause panic. I need to end this now before your mother or the Summer Lady finds out Commander Hardy has been bound by law. I know why he did what he did."

She opened her mouth and I shook my head. "I don't condone it one bit. Poor Ember was terrified, but it could have been worse if she hadn't found a way back into the world, she could have been lost forever. But I'm afraid of what the Queens might do to the man."

She glared at the wall, her eyes crackling with icy fire and she calmed herself. "I feel the same, the poor girl is just a baby... but I understand that the Fae cannot just run roughshod over the law as they did in a bygone era. We are part of this world and we need to abide by the laws of the land."

I nodded and said, "I promise... I'll head right home to bed after I get debriefed and I speak with the Queens in Flame's pen."

She froze and blinked at me. I smirked and pointed out, "There are only so many places you can hide Mab from Mother's eyes and sensors. And I know she wouldn't be foolish enough to return to Ha'real."

The woman smiled slowly and shook her head as she said, "If I weren't so mad at you right now, I'd find the way your mind works very sexy right now."

I grinned and then looked down at the smock I was wearing. "Or my impeccable style?"

She smiled and fought off a chuckle. Good, I wasn't up shit creek as far as I thought if I could get a smile out of her. I chanced it and leaned in as she lowered the ice barrier, and she started to move in too then her eyes locked on something behind me and she held a hand up between our lips.

Whaaaa? I glanced back to see Myra watching us, a crooked smirk on her lips. I sighed heavily as Rory stepped past me, knocking my shoulder as she hissed at me, "Commander Udriel?" And she was gone in a huff.

Graz zipped to my shoulder and whispered in my ear, "You're in it hip deep now Shade. Greater Fae are majorly territorial, and you had just come to an understanding that the two of you were courting. You shouldn't be hanging out with other potential mates, don't you know anything?"

I sputtered to her and to the Winter Maiden, "I didn't call her, Mother keeps doing it!"

She stopped next to Myra, who dipped gracefully into a respectful mini curtsy. "Majesty."

Aurora looked her up and down again then just nodded to herself once before saying, "I guess I owe you a debt of gratitude for watching my girl's back for me."

Myra just waved it off, tail twitching. "It's made things interesting for the last twenty-four hours. More entertaining than staring off into the dark waiting for sensor contact of things in the world's path."

Then she asked as I reached them and tried to drag Rory away physically, "So does she still do that thing when she kisses... with her toes?"

Aurora nodded as her glare turned into a smirk. "She scrunches them. Did she ever..."

I blurted, "Ok, that's enough of that, no time to compare notes. I've got to get some new gear and get this case closed. Come along your princess-ness." I marched right out, Graz opting to sit on Rory's pointed ear to listen to the two gossips until my girl felt I had suffered enough and followed after me.

I grumped, "I didn't call her!"

"So you keep on saying."

Before I knew it, we were in her personal white sports skiff with her guards driving. I let her know as much as I could about an open case, and kept insisting I needed to finish it. She relented to my insistence and that's how I found myself at the Beta-C Brigade headquarters in Irontown a few minutes later, with Zak just blinking at the torn-up mess that used to be the most advanced magi-tech scatter armor the Brigade had.

He muttered as he sifted through the mess with his two ancillary cybernetic arms while he crossed his other arms across his chest. "Damn it, Shade! This was R&D's experimental shit, it hadn't been permanently assigned to us yet." He looked over the helmet we found in the Ready Squadron landing bay on our way out of it. "At least this is still salvageable."

I squinted an eye in apology. "I have to go get my ass reamed by the brass, Zak, is there any way you could front me another set of SAs until I can requisition some?"

He huffed as the racks that held the Scatter Armor and other equipment started rotating past him. "Just one of the gauntlets with those nano-panels cost more than our combined yearly incomes, times two! Do you want to know what an entire gear-out cost?"

I winced, not wanting an answer to his hopefully rhetorical question. "A lot?"

"A shit ton of a lots!" He slowed at some armor that looked to be stained in greens and browns and smirked. "I oughta stick you with Freel's old SAs, but he's twice your size."

Eww... not that I have anything against water goblins, but they secrete a greenish-yellow puss from their pores that allows them to swim through the water much faster. But it smells like rotted algae and it stains everything and is almost impossible to wash out.

"Oh come on, Zak, you know you're my guy. I love you, man."

He sighed then smirked and then reached under his counter. "You're just damn lucky the geeks up in Research and Development find your feedback on that experimental armor invaluable and fascinating. Especially how you can over-stress it and even use it for things they hadn't even thought it could."

He placed a wire basket in front of me. "I was about to ship this up-ring to you before the fire. They have the next iteration of the armor with the tweaks you recommended as well as some additional enhancements they want you to evaluate for them."

I told him. "One thing you could pass along before my weekly armor evaluation report is that when the armor reconfigures into emergency EVA mode, it cuts off access to my gear. It almost cost me my life today."

He looked me up and down, taking in the medical smock and nodded. "I saw the reports. Damn Shade, you got a death wish or something? At this rate, you'll never make it to retirement."

"Well, I didn't start out the day thinking about how much fun it would be to get my ass kicked up on top of the world."

Zak shook his head as I slipped into the fresh set of sensor contact garments from the gear. "Didn't look like they kicked your ass from what I saw."

As I flexed in the skinsuit before donning the new armor I pointed to where Rory was pacing by the elevators. "Took all the king's horses, all the king's men, and a princess from the Unseelie Court to put me back together again."

The man snorted and I winked at him as he asked, "Well then, how do I requisition one of them?"

I put the helmet on, then flexed in the armor and cycled it, training it to my skin responses and my neural pathways. It seemed to be a little more responsive than the last, and I didn't get vertigo as its surface thought scanning software interfaced with me. I almost panicked the first time I tried some of this experimental bullshit.

Then I asked, "I don't suppose..." He rolled his eyes and slid another basket to me. A full loadout of gear for my belt including not one but two MMG guns, like I preferred. Then I sifted through the mess of the destroyed armor, looking for something. I smiled when my fingers closed over smooth, cold metal. I pulled out the harmonica Mac had gifted me and slid it into one of my new belt pouches.

The silver instrument gleamed in the light, looking brand new and untouched by the chaos which had destroyed the SAs. Of course, it wasn't damaged. If I were right about it, it held more power in it than any magi-tech tool available to the citizens of the Leviathan. And if my hunch was right, it was sort of a focus, to enhance any magics that flowed through it to amplify them tenfold.

Another reason I suspected Mac of not being who he said. But we both pretended that he really wasn't Rory's dad. King Oberon was dead after all, isn't that what all the Fae myths say?

I sighed and said, "Thank's Zak, you're the man. Now I have to..."

He was looking at the duty roster scrolling on his wall and said, "You apparently have to get your un-modded ass to Verd'real to meet with Reise, President Yang, and Queen Titania... like yesterday."

I groaned. Fuck me sideways and space me naked. Couldn't they just wait a couple of hours for me to wrap up the case in a pretty bow?

The old Human just chuckled at me. "That's why it pays to stay invisible, Knith."

"Yeah, yeah..." I flipped him off with a smile before trudging down the hall to tell Rory the bad news.

She was not happy, and my offer for her to accompany me was declined. Though I viewed her as one of the more enlightened of the Fae lords and ladies, the grudge between the courts was a palpable thing, and she didn't wish to be seen in the Summer Lady's palace.

So we agreed to meet at... home, after I got done with them and with my case. She reminded me I promised dinner. "Of course, I wouldn't miss it for the world." Then I tried to be funny. "Should we invite Myra?"

I could hear Graz slap her forehead from across the room as she groaned. Did I mention how I wasn't such a smooth operator? Yeah... there it was. I squeaked out, "Too soon?"

She pointed at the door then turned her back and I trudged past and to the lifts. I was going to pay for that tonight wasn't I? Ok, I saw a tiny quirk of her lip as the lift doors closed between us. The old Shade charm at work right there. That or she had gas, but I'd prefer the former.

Mother shattered my delusions by tsking and sighing out, "Oh Knith..." Then she played a song from the archives called Viva la Vida by a band known as Coldplay.

"Are you trying to tell me something?"

"Yes, I'm better at dating than you."

"But you've never been... on... a... you smartass."

"Guilty as charged."

By the time I was raked over the coals in the form of congratulating me for exposing the guilty parties and informed that the higher-ups would handle the closure of the case. The President awarded me the White Cross of the Leviathan for going above and beyond... basically a not so subtle way of telling me to keep my mouth shut about certain particulars of the case they didn't wish getting out to the public.

Later in a public ceremony, I would be awarded another heart medallion for being injured in the line of duty to go with my growing collection of them. Does it speak poorly of my competence if I keep getting injured?

I understood by the time I was allowed to leave that I was to be a good little Enforcer and keep my mouth shut. I did see something I didn't like in Titania's eyes when they spoke of having Max in custody. My lip burned as her eyes flared an angry flame. I needed to get her and Mab alone to warn them against doing anything drastic.

But just then, I was beyond exhausted, I just wanted to go home, have dinner with my girl, and sleep for a week. I let auto-nav on my Tac-Bike take me home while I napped.

When I arrived, Rory was there looking radiant in jeans and a tee, making the casual civilian garb look elegant and sexier than hells. She smiled bashfully and held her hands out from her sides and asked, "You like?"

I was just trying not to drool as I nodded. She dragged me over to sit. And there was a small cupcake sitting on a plate there. After she gave me a kiss that was so heated my ancestors could have felt it. She said, "Happy Birthday, Knith."

Then Graz and her family buzzed out of the bedchamber, holding a sign that seemed to be made of gossamer silk that said, "Happi Burthdae!" They all squeaked, "Happy Birthday!"

Graz squinted an eye. "The kids made the banner. We're trying to teach them to read and write like me." I blinked. Virtually no Sprites could read or write, most Fae think it is a waste of time to teach a race of 'vermin'. Whereas just about every other sentient race enrolls their children in the public schools. But none of the schools are equipped for children so small that another child accidentally sitting on them would kill them.

I couldn't stop smiling. I hadn't celebrated a birthday since I was enrolled in the academy... I never really had many friends once I graduated, and since I had no family, I didn't ever really pay attention to the date. "Is it really my birthday? Children, it's amazing, thank you."

Mother scrolled the date in my helmet before I took it off. Sure enough. This was the day they pulled me from the artificial womb in the Reproduction Clinic forty... seven years ago now. I would be almost a quarter of the way through my life, as the expected lifespan of humans is only two hundred. But I... was different... and technically won't ever look a day older.

Rory said as she took my helmet from my hands and set it down,

"Of course it is your birthday, silly woman. I would know." Yes, she would.

Then she held up the cupcake and with a whisper of magic an icy blue flame lit it. She smiled and said almost breathily, "Make a wish."

I looked around and realized I was growing my very own unorthodox family around me. What more was there to wish for? I shrugged and blew the candle out and the children went buzzing around like hyperactive sparkly lights as they cheered.

Twinkle buzzed up in front of me and I put my hand out and she landed on it, her eyes wide in wonder. "What did ya wish fer, Aunty Knith? I gots no birthdays yet."

I smiled at her and whispered like it were a big secret, "I can't tell you or it won't come true."

She nodded wisely then buzzed away, leaving a sprinkling of glowing dust behind.

Rory cleared her throat and looked plaintively at Graz. Our Sprite companion grabbed her two mate's hands and whistled. "Come on kids, I'll show you how to hotwire a mag-sled. I mean... let's go get some ice cream!"

They all cheered and in a trail of sifting dust up to a ceiling grill, they vanished into the ductwork, leaving me standing bashfully in front of Civilian Rory v1.0.

She smiled seductively and said, "I got you a gift?"

I almost asked, "Really?" But she placed a sparkly silver bow with trailing curly ribbons on top of her head as she advanced on me, whispering, "Mother, privacy mode."

Best birthday, ever!

EPILOGUE

As I sat around the card table in Mac's cabin on the Underhill a few weeks later, I said as I arranged the cards in my hand, the others watching my face intently for any tells, "You know Mac, my girl, the Winter Maiden, says she'd like to meet you. I'm always sneaking off every week to play cards and her curiosity is growing."

He was more intent than normal as he looked at his cards like they might change right before his eyes as he tried not to react. Instead, he said like it were of no consequence, "Is that so? And what did you tell her?"

He looked up at me and I could almost feel the weight of eons on me. I shrugged as I tossed one card to Mir, who was the dealer this round. "One." Then I looked at him. "I said I'd have to check with you but I was sure it was no problem. It isn't is it? A problem?"

He narrowed his eyes at me as we played a game other than the card game we were participating in, "Why would it be a problem?"

I shrugged as everyone discarded and got new cards. Mir really had to dial back her reactions in her emotional response software, as one of her mirrored eyes ticked.

Ben always had such a pained and pensive look whenever he organized his cards like it were such a serious task. That's how he was when on duty as an enforcer. I certainly hope he didn't use that look in the brothel where he worked for some extra chit to supplement his income.

Jane always folded when things got too rich. She just watches with her big doe eyes blinking, it was what made her Faun race so damn cute. But don't let that fool you, as she also ran the brothel here on the Underhill and was a shrewd businesswoman.

I prompted the old captain, "So it's ok then?"

He rearranged his cards, the ironclad control he usually had over his facial expression strained from the topic giving me insight into his hand. It was decent and he was scheming like a Fae to leverage the most profit out of it. "I don't see why it wouldn't be... just clear it with me to make sure I'm in when she comes."

Our new sixth, who Rory was no longer jealous of once she found she was dating some half-elf twins, Raliegh and Monica... Myra had a tell... I mean tail. Whenever she was excited about a hand, the end of her tail would twitch. Everyone but Mir had figured that out already. The Sentinel pilot was all twitch, twitch as she asked everyone else, "Are these two playing the same thing as us?"

Mir snuggled up to her because she says Myra's fur feels sinful against her mirrored skin. "Just ignore them. They're always double-talking around us. We're just waiting for the day Knith grows a pair and just accuses the old fart plainly what it is they dance around."

I've had a feeling since day one, that Mir knew the answers to all the questions and suspicions I had about who Mac really was. I was like ninety-five percent sure I was correct. But I found myself acting more and more like the Fae as I hung around with them.... and I enjoyed the game.

I was sure if I called before we came, Mac, who never seemed to leave the Underhill, would be out on errands, but I also saw the eyes of a man who wished to see his daughter. I wondered if Rory could see through the glamour to the man beneath and recognize him. Odds were about even and I think he knew that, since if he was Oberon, his bastard son, Lord Sindri hadn't seen through it.

I've felt both Sin's and Rory's power, and I'm of the opinion she is more powerful than her half brother.

I shrugged and threw a full food ration card, ten chit, and a plasma capacitor in the middle as I said, "She really misses having a father and I'm sure that she'd be happy to see him if she ever met him again."

He just nodded and dropped five little bricks of trillium in the pot. After all bets were in, Ben folding, they showed their cards once I called their bets.

Mir squinted an eye and said almost in question, "Half moon?"

Mac patted her shoulder in a consoling manner and said to me, "Would she now?" Then to the room. "Two half-moons." His grin was predatory.

I whistled at that and Myra snickered and said "Sorry people, but mama needs a new scratching post. Three-quarter form," as she laid down her cards like a trophy cocking an eyebrow at me.

I sighed and said, "That is a hard hand to beat." She grinned in triumph as she reached for the trinkets in the middle of the table. And I laid my cards down on top of the pile to stop her, "Quad-form!"

They all moaned and she blurted, "Bullshit! Again? She has to be cheating."

Everyone was nodding in agreement as I raked in my winnings. Mac said, "We just can't figure out how."

I sighed. "I've told you all, each and every one of you has a tell."

Mir pointed to the only piece of clothing she wore, a purple tank top that looked about to tear as it stretched over her prodigious breasts. "I'm covered up, you can't see my cards anymore." Then accused, "There's no way you're reading Mac."

I smirked as I collected the cards and started to deal the next hand. "Actually his would be a reverse tell. You see, he plays like a Fae, I'm sure he learned that somewhere. And Fae are all about cunning deception, so if you go into a hand with that in mind..."

Myra nodded. "Don't play the man, play the cards." I tapped my nose and pointed at her.

Mac growled and grinned.

I looked around the table and marveled at my growing ring of friends. I had a family I chose now, and friends I held dear. My life had changed so drastically in the past few months, and as odd as it sounds, I feel... alive for the first time.

I thought back to the prior Friday, after Max's trial and sentencing to the mines two days prior and feeling I might not survive my confrontation with the Queens of the divided Courts.

It turns out Max hadn't been in on the attempt on my life, he had actually been preparing to turn himself into me for his involvement in the fire while the Alpha One Three crew ferried me out to look at the damaged area. He had figured I had put it all together. He didn't know I had a history with his accomplices.

He had learned of the secret airlock a year ago when that area suffered substantial meteoroid damage and his system came up flagged Double Black for the replacement panels. Finding out it had a camouflaged outer airlock door built into it.

He took a random crew and had them sign non-disclosures as per the instructions in the encrypted files. It was a Fae contract with the original External Maintenance Commanders, and breaching the contract would leave him subject to punishment by the Fae and the loss of the generous bonuses the Maintenance Commanders got at the end of each ship year. The only real positive of his position.

After removing the Skin scale he had gone in to inspect the superstructure for damage and looked through the inner airlock window to see the magic-induced world inside, and the Summer Queen with Ember.

It was after the new budget proposal was deferred so that the Fae could have yet another unnecessary perk installed in the upper rings, that he got frustrated. He was trying to revolutionize the way the

External Maintenance programs were run, and streamline and modernize all the procedures, but the rich people and Fae wanted a damn water feature.

And he knew as he ordered his crew to vent that pen, that it was the wrong thing to do. He tried reasoning with himself that it was only a stupid animal, not knowing it was sentient. But he had recently got a pet and knew how heartbreaking it would be to lose Spike. So he thought it would be a good way to punish Titania, and she wouldn't be able to report it lest she revealed that the Fae had hidden compartments on the Leviathan.

The only reason he even knew about it was the contingency plan that was in place just in case this exact scenario happened, where that portion of the Skin needed repair during the ten thousand year flight. Operational safety.

He changed his mind just after sending the crew of A13 out to do it, and he recalled them, but it was too late, they had done the deed. Only when the pen experienced explosive decompression, Ember hadn't been blown out into space. She had grabbed the seal of the airlock door and pulled herself onto the Skin, her claws burning through the hull, and she scrabbled until she found the other airlock and melted her way in.

By the gods, I can't imagine just how terrified the little one was.

The A13 crew replaced the scorched and damaged panels right after the fire was contained so that nobody would ask questions. Max said he was just waiting to be discovered and knew the first time I had talked to him that the jig was likely up because he said, "You didn't strike me as a half-assed investigator."

He had never imagined the sheer amount of damage that occurred when his plan went to hells. And he tried to rationalize that since nobody was killed, and he didn't think the Fae would admit to having a Firewyrm, that it would all just go away. It didn't.

Under pressure from the Seelie, Unseelie, and the President, it was a closed-door trial. Since our findings showed he hadn't been involved in the attempt on my life, and the three who had were dead anyway, that instead of arson, the charges would be a dereliction of duty and reckless negligence resulting in structural damage to the world.

Due in part to me suggesting a reduced sentence for the very competent Maintenance Commander, he was found guilty and sentenced to just a year in the pressurized side of the mines with the possibility of parole in six months.

I wound up responsible for finding a temporary home for Spike since Max was a Clinic Child like me and had no family. I gave him to Rory in my office outside of her lab with a smirk. The sneak had just smiled and said, "Nyx?"

Her poor personal assistant, who she has never used, had almost catapulted up from her desk, pen and paper in hand, ready to take a message. She deflated when she realized she wasn't needed for that when Rory asked her, "You like animals from what I hear when J'real is flirting with you. Could you please take care of this little one?"

Nyx had just about melted into a puddle as she accepted the pooch.

I had told Rory, "Sneak."

"Guilty as charged."

I'd never win.

I had been in a dark mood when Thursday, a report came across my desk about an industrial accident down in the mines. An unfortunate collapse of the tunnels had claimed Max's life and it had been determined by structural engineers that that portion of the asteroid, which served as the Heart of the Leviathan, had been over mined and the collapse was ruled an accident.

How can something in micro-gravity collapse? Especially now that the asteroid was over eighty percent mined out? There wouldn't be enough mass for hydrostatic equilibrium to be a factor, and even if it was, it wouldn't happen quick enough in microgravity to trap someone.

I knew what had truly happened and I wasn't happy about it. I went down there after the tunnels were deemed safe and found patches of ice along with patches of heated rock near where they found Max.

I had barged in on Mab in Flame's pen on Friday having Myra drop me off on the Skin and leave me there. Then after her Sentinel ship was out of sight, I entered the hidden airlock on Beta-B to find the same type of illusionary world. And Mab was shocked to see me there.

Flame... was huge compared to Ember, but had that same sort of childlike curiosity about her as she virtually flowed over the magical landscape to see me. I wonder if I was the first person she had ever seen on the world outside of the Queens.

As Mab was calling out as she stalked forward, "What are YOU doing here? And how did you get past the wards?" I was pulling out a couple of apples from my pouches to offer to the inquisitive Firewyrm.

She happily chomped them down and allowed me to place my hands on her muzzle as I got much more intelligible flashes from her. Curiosity. Name. Flame. Happy.

I grinned at her and placed my forehead on her and said, "Hello Flame, I'm Knith. It's such a pleasure to meet you. I know your little sister, Ember."

A lot of excited and happy impressions flashed. She missed her sister and liked hearing about how she was doing. I'm assuming nobody told her that they almost lost Ember recently.

Mab looked almost shocked to see me communicating with Flame, then she narrowed her eyes at me to start a tirade. I wasn't in the mood, a good man was dead, and every bone in my body told me the Queens had gone after him for endangering Ember. I also knew it would be futile to investigate it as they had already had the engineers sign off on the collapse, and unless I could prove the hot and cold areas were from their magics, it would likely be the end of my career.

I held up a finger as I gently stroked Flame's muzzle, and I said in a cold but pleasant tone as not to alarm Flame, "Don't even start with me. I'm not in the mood right now. Call your fellow nutcase queen, now. I've a few demands you need to address."

She started to hiss out some sort of threat, but I took a single step, so we were eye to eye, and I whispered, "Does it look like I'm playing around right now, Mab?"

She took a moment, then hesitated as I glared at her. She didn't break eye contact as she made a motion with her hand. I could feel the magic pulse from her. A few moments later, Titania was stroking the side of Flame's face as she asked with concern, "What is it, Mab? Is Flame..."

Then she stopped and cocked an eyebrow when she started to turn and saw us. "This is interesting. What exactly is..."

I held a finger up toward her, refusing to be the one to break eye contact first. "I'll get to you in a second."

She opened her mouth, looking incensed, then looked at Mab and me again and cocked her head like she was looking for something. Mab just huffed and took a step back, looking past me. "The enforcer says that she has some demands of the 'nutcase' queens."

They chuckled together as Titania stepped beside her so she could study me more intensely. "My mark on her is fading already. How do you... wait, you reinforce yours from time to time, don't you? Partial magic immunity is dangerous. How have you allowed her to survive this long? So many of the magical races would have a target on her head if they learned of it."

"My daughter has taken an interest in her. And I do find her interesting myself."

I sighed and said, "Shut up, both of you." They blinked at me in unison, as if I had just slapped them.

Mab said coolly, "Mind yourself, Shade, or you'll find yourself decorating my bedchambers."

"Stow the threats, I know what you did. What little respect and fear I had for the two of you has evaporated into the ether."

Titania started, "What is it that you think..."

I cut her off, "I don't think you did it, I know you did it. But what I know and what I can prove are two different things. So here we are. I just want you to know that you don't fool everyone. He was a good man who made a bad choice. And he was paying for that choice."

They looked at each other with virtually identical scheming looks on their faces. I didn't let them start playing their Fae games, I just pushed forward, "This is what is going to happen. First, you are going to find the funding to implement all the changes that Commander Hardy had requested for the External Maintenance Crew. Including raises. Not just for his stack but for all four stacks."

"He had good ideas, great foresight, and the good of the world in mind. Now we'll never know if he could have made up for his one moment of weakness."

The Summer Lady was grinning now, "You expect us to find funding for..."

I stopped her, "I'm not done." I pulled out a pad and handed it to them, Mab took it as they looked down at the contents displayed on it. "In all their wisdom, the department of finance took it upon themselves to bill me for the 'perfectly good antenna system' that I tore up to defend myself when I was investigating who had done this to Ember. You're paying for it."

Mab started, "What makes you think..."

"Thumbprint."

They looked at each other and their amusement was fading, then Titania slowly reached over and placed her thumb on the pad. I grinned and took it from them, and before they could speak, I continued, "And lastly, you'll adjust your wards to allow me and the Sprite, Graz, to visit Ember and Flame whenever we like. The girls are lonely and seeing only you, and I would assume one or two of your children, is not enough. They've been in isolation for five thousand years. They need more time to play and interact with others."

They sat in silence looking at me, assuring themselves I was done before Mab asked tongue in cheek, "And what makes you believe we will acquiesce to any of these demands by a mere human?"

My eyes narrowed and I let all my rage and frustration and guilt burn in my eyes and they both actually took a half step back when I stepped up to them, "Because, my dear Queens. This mere human will make it her life's work to investigate not only the death of Max Hardy, but every shady dealing the Seelie and Unseelie Courts have ever had, and any questionable activity by any of the Greater Fae."

"And from what Aurora tells me, my life has the potential to be very long, and I intend to be a thorn in your side for the full extent of it. And before you get any ideas... a Commander of the External Maintenance Crew can meet with an untimely death, especially one who was a Clinic Child who has no family, without many questions being asked."

I gave them a predatory smile. "And it is an entirely different thing for a decorated Lieutenant of the Enforcer's Brigade who has been awarded the White Cross of the Leviathan to vanish without a trace. Especially if that same Enforcer had the forethought to keep a record of all my dealings and suspicions with the Fae royalty offsite somewhere in case of such a disappearance."

Titania turned to Mab and said, "I may have just orgasmed a little. I think I'm in love with this one."

Mab smirked at her and said, "You couldn't handle her, Tina. Besides, my Rory has a thing for the brash girl. But she truly is fascinating, isn't she? She plays the game like a true Fae."

Then to me, she said, "Without admitting any culpability, we will accept your deal, Knith Shade of the Beta-Stack A-Ring. But heed our word that threatening the Summer and Winter Ladies is not something we can let pass, and we will rectify the situation ourselves if you feel the need to do it again. Are we clear on this?"

I nodded. "Crystal." That's when my relief that they agreed caused my adrenaline induced courage to crumble. I was scared shitless at the way I had dealt with them, but it had to be done.

Mab nodded and said as she grabbed the back of my head, "Sealed with a kiss." I gasped and stumbled, my body feeling as though it had been frozen from the inside out when she released me after searing my soul with her magic again.

Before I could catch my breath, the iron grip of Queen Titania pulled me to her as she said, "Sealed with a kiss." I was screaming into her mouth as she seared every cell with the hot fire of her magic. I could feel my lips were fire and ice, sizzling and one eye felt hot, the other chilled as she dropped me to collapse on the fake moss beneath us.

Titania just took Mab's hand and they took a step forward and were gone, the Summer Lady had teleported them away, leaving me there, a drooling mess in Flame's pen. The Firewyrm projected amusement as she licked the side of my head with her huge tongue.

I shook the memory out of my head. It had taken me almost an hour before I had the strength to stand and get myself out of there lest they return. Just the memory had one of my eyes icing over and the other flickering with magical fire.

It had been only a couple of hours after the showdown when an anonymous donor had quadrupled the budget for the External Maintenance Crews for the duration of the flight so that everything Max had wanted would be implemented, including raises. The staffing would double as well as the stipend to pay the day jobbers.

Mac was looking at me with concern. I smiled at him and shrugged, then said, "Ok... dealer takes two."

… then sirens and warning klaxons started sounding. These were different than any I have ever heard as we all stood up from the table. I grabbed Myra's old goggles and put them on, asking, "Mother, what is it?"

She forgot to sound mechanical as she voiced in what sounded like a stunned tone, "Proximity alert. Unknown ships are on approach."

I blinked. Ships? What? Mab's tits! We were literally in the middle of interstellar space.

Fuck me sideways and space me naked. May we live in interesting times.

The End

Books in the Worldship Files series...
Leviathan
Firewyrm
Cityships (2020)

Books in the Techromancy Scrolls series...
Adept
Soras
Masquerade
Westlands
Avalon
New Cali
Colossus (2020)

Books in the Urban Fairytales series...
Red Hood: The Hunt
Snow: The White Crow
Ella: Cinders and Ash
Rose: Briar's Thorn
Let Down Your Hair
Hair of Gold: Just Right
The Hood of Locksley
Beauty In the Beast
No Place Like Home
Shadow Of The Hook
Armageddon

Books in the New Sentinels series...
Djinn: Cursed
Raven Maid: Out of the Darkness
Fate: No Strings Attached
Open Seas: Just Add Water
Ghost-ish: Lazarus
Anubis: Death's Mistress
Sentinels: Reckoning (2020)

Books in the Drakon series...
Awakening
Dragonfall

Books in the Valkyrie Chronicles series...
Return of the Asgard
Bloodlines
Folkvangr
Seventy Two Hours
Titans

Books in the Tales From Olympus series...
Gods Reunited
Alfheim
Odyssey (2020)

Books in the Bridge series...
Trolls
Traitor
Unbroken

Books in the Fracture series...
Divergence

Novellas by Erik Schubach

The Hollow

Novellas in the Paranormals series...
Fleas
This Sucks
Jinx (2020)

Novellas in the Fixit Adventures...
Fixit
Glitch
Vashon
Descent
Sedition (2020)

Novellas in the Emily Monroe Is Not The Chosen One series...
Night Shift
Unchosen
Rechosen (2020)

Short Stories by Erik Schubach
(These short stories span many different genres)

A Little Favor
Lost in the Woods
MUB
Mirror Mirror On The Wall
Oops!
Rift Jumpers: Faster Than Light
Scythe
Snack Run
Something Pretty

Books in the Music of the Soul universe...
(All books are standalone and can be read in any order)
Music of the Soul
A Deafening Whisper
Dating Game
Karaoke Queen
Silent Bob
Five Feet or Less
Broken Song
Syncopated Rhythm
Progeny
Girl Next Door
Lightning Strikes Twice
June
Dead Shot

Music of the Soul Shorts...
(All short stories are standalone and can be read in any order)
Misadventures of Victoria Davenport: Operation Matchmaker
Wallflower
Accidental Date
Holiday Morsels
What Happened In Vegas?

Books in the London Harmony series...
(All books are standalone and can be read in any order)
Water Gypsy
Feel the Beat
Roctoberfest
Small Fry
Doghouse
Minuette
Squid Hugs
The Pike
Flotilla

Books in the Pike series...
(All books are standalone and can be read in any order)
Ships In The Night
Right To Remain Silent
Evermore
New Beginnings

Books in the Flotilla series...
(All books are standalone and can be read in any order)
Making Waves
Keeping Time
The Temp
Paying the Toll

Books in the Unleashed series...
Case of the Collie Flour
Case of the Hot Dog
Case of the Gold Retriever
Case of the Great Danish
Case of the Yorkshire Pudding
Case of the Poodle Doodle
Case of the Hound About Town
Case of the Shepherd's Pie

Printed in Great Britain
by Amazon